Southern Swamps and Ruins

21 haunting tales by

Richard D. Laudenslager
and
Fran Rizer

with guest authors

L. Michelle Cox
Jenifer Boone Lybrand
Nathan R. Rizer
J. Michael Shell
Robert Simkins
Two Ravens

First Print Edition March, 2016

Odyssey South Publishing and logo are trademarks of Odyssey South Publishing.

This book is a work of fiction. Names, characters, places, and incidents are products of the authors' imaginations or are used fictitiously.

ISBN-13: 978-0692619445
ISBN-10: 0692619445

CONTENTS

PART ONE — INTO THE SWAMP

TWO - MILE SWAMP

By Richard D. Laudenslager

PART TWO — THROUGH THE SWAMP

By Fran Rizer

PART THREE — OUT OF THE SWAMP

By Guest Authors

PART FOUR — ABOUT THE AUTHORS

Part One

INTO THE SWAMP

Two - Mile Swamp

RICHARD D. LAUDENSLAGER

INTRODUCTION

By *Richard D. Laudenslager*

AS A KID growing up in the 70s, my friends and I spent most of our waking hours outdoors. We played lots of sports including basketball with a hoop my father hung over our garage. Three friends and I made our own baseball field in a vacant lot behind one of their houses and invited other kids from the neighborhood to play with us. We had to clear weeds for the bases and trample the baselines to see where we were running.

Our football field was another vacant lot filled with stump holes—hidden little voids that collapsed when your foot hit them. They added that extra element of danger known as the twisted ankle. Good old-fashioned hit 'em hard tackle football where you walked away with at least a few bruises and chances were you skinned a knee or elbow, too. Maybe got a bloody-nose, or the occasional headache, probably from mild concussions.

We played hide and seek, no explanation necessary. No man stands, self-explanatory. And chase, for goodness sake. Chase—a game where all we did was run after one another. During the summers, we each adopted a summer name. Mine was Diesel Daddy. I was a big boy.

We climbed trees. Well, my friends climbed trees. I rooted them on from below—again, big boy. We rode bikes together for miles and miles, walked marathon distances, and never tired. We kept snakes as pets, mostly hognose or the occasional green snake, and played with them, got bitten by them. We swam in creeks with crayfish—and worse—and played in mud holes. We shot each other with bb guns. Not the kind they have today, but the ones you cocked once like a Winchester rifle. Those shots didn't break the skin, but they still hurt like heck. Lastly, or at least the last thing I remember, we'd sneak up on one another with a handful of Devil's Spears, a thin grass-like plant with needle-sharp tips and throw them into someone's back. I have no idea what the real name was, but they hurt like heck, too.

My point is, we lacked the modern conveniences and distractions computers, electronic game consoles, television, and texting has become to our children today. Oh, we had television, four whole channels that played from 6 a.m. to 12 p.m. Yeah, kids—our parents didn't have to shut off the TV for us. The networks did it. What we did have in great abundance was imagination—the kind that turned sticks into swords, hammers into guns, cardboard boxes into forts—and the swamp into a mysterious place filled with monsters. Except . . . we discovered the monsters were real.

WRETCHED RUDY

IT WAS EARLY in the summer of 1977 when I turned eleven years old. That's not true. Actually, by the calendar, it was late spring. May, to be specific, but I don't care what the calendar says, when you're WAeleven, and school is out for the year, it's summer.

As birthdays go, turning eleven is a fairly unremarkable event in one's life when you consider that just one year earlier I had achieved an epic milestone — ten years old — double freaking digits. The realization there would now be a one in front of my age for the next nine years was awe-inspiring. I mean — wow. Then as eleven approached, it dawned on me there were two — whole — long — years ahead of me before I would reach the vaunted realm of teenager. With that thought in mind, my eleventh birthday quickly lost what little magic it had held for me. That was, until late one evening, sitting in front of the television, I discovered there was a Galaxy far, far away.

Star Wars was coming to a drive-in near me, the deep voice emanating from the television had informed me, and by God I was going to be there to see it. So, that night, I asked my mother if she would take my three best friends—Ronald, Donnie, Toad—and me to Ray's Drive-In in Lexington that weekend to celebrate my birthday. She agreed, and my birthday was magical once more.

Ronald and Donnie were pretty normal guys but Toad was a wee bit different. His real name was Herbert, but he hated that name. We had tried calling him Herb, Bert, Herbie, and even Robert, but he didn't like any of those either. Then, one day, we caught him trying to get high by licking the belly of a toad, so we took to calling him Toad. For some reason, he liked that, so it stuck.

At that time, nothing beat going to the drive-in with a few buddies on a balmy summer evening. The key was to get there early enough to pick the perfect spot with the best view of the screen—not too close and not too far away. Once we had staked our claim to a perfect little island of land in the center of the huge theater parking lot, we unfolded our lawn chairs, laid out blankets, and sat under the stars waiting for the movie to start. All was good until someone whipped the chair out from under Toad's butt as he sat back, sending him hard to the ground. It was Buddy and Daniel, who was Donnie's older brother.

"Leave us alone!" yelled Ronald, shoving at Buddy in the process, only to be sidestepped and sent to the ground himself, eating a mouthful of dirt for his effort.

"You guys are pathetic with your lawn chairs and blankets," said Buddy. "I'll bet one of your mommies dropped you off, didn't they?" he finished sarcastically, looking back at a grinning Daniel.

"No," said Ronald, pushing up on his palms and spitting bits of dirt and grass out of his mouth as he glared at Buddy. "Richard's brother did," he continued, cocking his head in my direction. "He's getting us some hotdogs from concessions right now. I imagine he'll be back *any* minute."

At that, Buddy's mood soured quickly, and after a couple wide-eyed head jerks to check all directions, Daniel suggested they get the heck out of there. And they did.

Donnie helped Toad, who was grimacing and rubbing his tailbone vigorously, get to his feet. I reached out a hand to Ronald and pulled him up. He spat one last wad of dirt out of his mouth, then grinned wide, obviously pleased with himself for scaring off Buddy and Daniel.

"Grin all you want now," I said, "but what happens when Buddy figures out it was my mom, and not my brother, who brought us here?"

Ronald laughed hard and said, "After what your brother did to him two years ago, he's probably going to leave this place figuring if we talk about what just happened, your brother will kick his ass all the way back to Two-Mile Swamp."

The four of us were more like brothers than friends. Hardly a day passed when we did not spend at least part of it together—always having fun, watching each other's backs, and probably annoying the hell out of the people around us. I was the youngest; Ronald, a year older; and Donnie and Toad, two years older than me. They tolerated me because I was a big boy, bigger than any of them, and the fact my family had a swimming pool might have had a little to do with it. It was a different time, a time without video games, without cell phones, and without all the distractions caused by the Internet. We actually had to invent our own fun. Imagine that! Other than sleeping, eating, and school, we probably spent ninety percent of our waking hours playing outdoors.

Although, during the summer, sleeping and eating were always optional.

It was not long before we were glued to the giant screen as it lit up, whisking us away to a far, far away galaxy where an amazing adventure unfolded before our very eyes. I remember thinking this was the greatest movie I'd ever seen.

The four of us stayed captivated and amazed throughout the entire film. By the time we left Ray's Drive-In that night, we were convinced our summer had already peaked — and that nothing, nothing at all, could top that night.

Of that, we would be mistaken.

The next morning found the four of us sitting on the old wooden trestle that spanned the nearly dry Rutherford Creek bed below us. It was definitely not the safest place for a group of young boys to hang out, but it was where we spent a great deal of time. In the winter and spring months, Rutherford Creek flowed freely, lapping at its banks, making the trestle a tempting diving platform, but during the summer, the creek narrowed to barely more than a trickle. Still, we spent many hours climbing through the crisscrossed timbers or sitting on the trestle, dangling our feet through the wooden ties, tossing rocks into what remained of the Rutherford.

The trestle was the gateway to Two-Mile Swamp.

"Do you know the legend of Wretched Rudy?" Donnie asked me.

"Nope, tell it," I said. Donnie had a gift when it came to telling stories. He was really smart and mature for his age, and could make them sound just like he was reading a book to us.

"Not that load of crap again," Ronald said. "Haven't we heard that story enough?"

"I haven't." I said, looking at Ronald.

"Let him tell it." Toad said, eying Ronald, too. "It's a good story, and Donnie tells it better than any of us."

"Oh, all right," Ronald said with a huff.

"During the late 1800s," Donnie began, "a wicked little train conductor used the local rail line to further his own interests by smuggling cargo along the route he was assigned. He would sneak his contraband aboard at scheduled stops, then bring the train to a halt along the stretch of tracks that crossed a desolate breadth of land known as Two-Mile Swamp.

"This portion of the tracks was built atop a towering earthen berm that cut a scar across the face of the dense swamp. Over the years, the north side of the railway berm had dried up, and thick, thorny briars had grown to blanket the landscape beneath, making it nearly impassable while the swamp thrived on the southern side."

Donnie hacked loudly, cleared his throat, and continued, "In this area, far away from prying eyes, the conductor's pack of thieves had blazed a trail through the thick carpet of briars north of the swamp and they would lie in wait in the shadows of the looming berm.

"Once the conductor had brought the column of cars to a stop near the midpoint of Two-Mile Swamp, he would exit the train, and then make his way along the tracks with his twisted, mahogany walking stick gripped tightly in his bony fingers. The metal-tipped staff would cast off tiny bursts of light as it sparked when striking the gravel base beneath the tracks. The sound of metal on rock and the eerie sizzling created by the sparks shredded the still night air, beckoning the conductor's approach to the cadre of men awaiting his signal. After eyeing the length of the tracks in both directions, the conductor would rap his walking stick three times against the wooden boxcar to declare the coast was clear.

"I've never heard all that detail about the walking stick before," Toad said, wide-eyed.

"Yeah, where'd that come from?" Ronald asked sarcastically.

"Who cares," I said. "It's cool, let him finish."

"Thank you," Donny said with a satisfied nod, cleared his throat, and continued.

"Having heard the signal, shadowy figures would ascend from the shrouded depths beneath the tracks to do the conductor's bidding. He would oversee the off-loading of the specified cargo, all the while sneering and casting biting insults at the men to hasten their pace. The thieves would then lower the haul down the steep, treacherous embankment and into an awaiting wagon.

"With the task completed, the bandits would dissolve back into the dark abyss as the conductor crawled back aboard the train to signal the engineer to get under way.

"But, one particular summer evening found the regular brakeman suddenly ill, and a young Rudy Mann was tasked to take his place in the caboose. A last-minute replacement, Rudy had barely caught the train before it left the station, and he was unable to alert the conductor about the change. With his wife in the midst of labor, Rudy had lingered at home as long as he could with the midwife at her side to await the birth of his first child. The last thing he wanted to do was leave his young love at this most precious time, but having just landed the brakeman's job, he agreed with his wife that he needed to go to work. With one hand placed tenderly on her swollen belly, Rudy leaned in to give his wife a gentle kiss. She smiled softly back at him, suppressing the urge to cry.

"Oh. My. God!" Ronald said, dragging the words out, burying his face in his hands, and making a disgusting sound like he was about to puke.

"Shut up! I said to Ronald, as Donnie shot me a thankful look and continued the story.

"'It's a short loop, my dear,' Rudy said to her as he smiled and looked into her watery deep-blue eyes, 'with any luck, I'll be back before the baby arrives.' They both drew short, excited breaths and beamed with joy when the baby delivered a vigorous kick where Rudy's hand rested.

"A wide smile parted Rudy's wife's face, and with joyful tears streaming down her rosy cheeks, she said, 'I don't think the baby wants you to go either.'"

"Do you have to tell all that mushy stuff?" Toad complained.

"Quiet!" I said, wanting to hear the whole story. "I swear if one of you opens your trap again, I'm going to put my fist in it!"

"Thank you, again," Donnie said narrowing his eyes at Toad as he went on with the story. "As the train departed, Rudy's thoughts were elsewhere. He recalled that in his haste to leave the house, he had left a note the regular brakeman had passed to him through the messenger that had informed him of the man's illness. Never having opened the letter, Rudy would never see its simple instruction: *Do not, under any circumstances, leave the caboose.*

"It was nearly midnight when the conductor ordered the train to come to a halt on the barren stretch of tracks in the middle of Two-Mile Swamp. Rudy, prompted by the unscheduled stop, exited the caboose to see what the trouble was. With only his brakeman's signal lantern and its faint red glow to guide him, Rudy could hardly see the barely illuminated, narrow, graveled fringe between the train and the perilous slope to his right.

"Rudy made his way cautiously along the tracks in the shadow of the railcars as an odd, clicking sound in the distance drew his attention. All at once, three loud taps of wood striking wood broke the silent, still evening air. Rudy hastened his pace toward the source of the clamor, the burning lantern washing out before him. As he rounded the bend in the rail line, he was astonished to see a grim little fellow overseeing a small group of men removing some wooden crates from the train. Before he could question what was happening, the menacing gang of thugs spotted Rudy and darted in his direction, surrounding him.

"Rudy tried to turn on his heels and retreat to the caboose, but two enormous, burly men quickly restrained him.

"'You're the conductor,' said Rudy, completely puzzled by his realization.

"The frail little man advanced, stabbed his metal-tipped staff into Rudy's chest, and, with a deep, contemptuous sigh, declared to the group, 'These are most unfortunate circumstances.'"

Donnie paused for a moment. "Go on," I urged him.

"Hold on," Donnie said. "My throat's dry." He spat across the trestle, and then went on, "The conductor ordered his brutes to take the brakeman to the opposite side of the tracks and drown him in the swamp. After crossing between the cars, Rudy tried to break free from the two beastly men restraining him, but the conductor struck him hard across his brow with the heavy, wooden walking stick. Dazed,

17

Rudy's legs collapsed beneath him, and he slumped to the ground. The conductor looked on, callously checking the time on his pocket watch, while his men beat Rudy savagely.

"Barely clinging to life, Rudy Mann lay beside the train in a crumpled mass. As the vile little conductor stepped to Rudy's side, the crunching sound of gravel filled his ears. Rudy's thoughts returned to his loving wife—and to the child she carried for him. Drawing upon his last remaining vestige of strength, Rudy peered up at the conductor through pleading, blood-soaked eyes. He tried to speak; struggling to form words with his mangled jaw and bloodied, shattered teeth, but all he could manage to do was mouth the word—*Please*.

"His broken jaw, crumbled teeth, and shredded swollen tongue made him impossible to under-stand—not that his plea would have changed anything. The conductor's response, a fiendish grin, was cast toward young Rudy as he buried the tip of his staff in the man's abdomen and pushed hard, sending Rudy's broken body tumbling down the steep, rocky slope and into the murky swamp water below.

"Rudy lay on his back, only partially submerged, mired in the thick, slimy liquid, struggling as much as his pain-wracked broken form would allow. For the men who watched and laughed grimly from the tracks above, only seconds passed—but it seemed like an eternity to Rudy. Overwrought with pain, Rudy forced one last agonizing scream. The bloodcurdling sound of his bellow seemingly emanated not from the man, but from somewhere else—somewhere—not of this world.

"The assembled men shuddered, a cold chill creeping up their spines, as they watched the swamp open up and swallow Rudy Mann."

"Ooooooh." Toad made a scary sound.

"For the love of Pete," I said, "be quiet and let him tell the story!"

Donnie huffed, rolled his eyes, and continued, "The conductor eyed the still burning brakeman's lantern lying at his feet, flipped the twisted staff in his hand to grasp the metal tip, then swung the curved, metal knob like a sickle at the lantern, snagged its handle, and brought it to him.

"As a final act of contempt toward the meddling young man, the conductor launched the lantern into the swamp where the brakeman's body had just been sucked under. Once again, that fiendish grin parted the conductor's thin lips, but it was just as quickly wiped clean from his face. Looking down upon the black water, he watched Rudy's hand erupt from murky water, clutch the lantern's handle, and drag it down into the depths with him.

"Visibly shaken by what they had just witnessed, the men hurriedly finished their task and sent the train on its way.

"As the legend goes, Rudy Mann was assumed lost as a result of a freak accident and his body never recovered. After a brief respite of his criminal activities, the conductor resumed his illicit ways, though not for long. Soon thereafter, his next late-night rendezvous would be his last. The authorities found the conductor's train abandoned on the tracks in Two-Mile Swamp. There was no sign of the crew and no evidence of what had happened to them. The investigation concluded the disappearances were the result of a botched robbery attempt, but nothing other than the crew was found to be missing."

"I'm telling you that story is crap!" Ronald said emphatically as Donnie finished telling the tale. "There's nothing haunting that swamp," he continued, pointing in the swamp's direction. "They're just trying to scare us."

"Who's trying to scare us?" I asked, never having heard the story before today.

"Who do you think?" Toad chimed in, rubbing his still tender tailbone from last night. "I first heard this story told by Buddy."

"Me, too," said Ronald. "It's just more of Buddy's bull ... "

"That's not true," Donnie interjected, cutting Ronald off before he could finish his thought. "My Uncle Bob worked for the railroad. He used to tell me and my brothers about the red light in the swamp all the time. He'd seen it!"

"You mean he said he'd seen it," Ronald added, sounding somewhat less annoyed now. "What he probably saw was swamp gas," he continued with a laugh, apparently amused at the thought. "That stuff gets blamed for everything from Bigfoot to ghosts and even UFOs."

"What about the grotesque figure roaming the tracks with the lantern?" Toad asked.

"He never mentioned any of that to us, and it wasn't swamp gas," Donnie said, looking at Ronald who rolled his eyes.

"That grotesque figure is more of Buddy's garbage," said Ronald, throwing up his hands in frustration. "I'm just saying," he continued, eyeing Donnie, "you don't really know what your uncle saw because you weren't there."

"And you don't know what he didn't see," Donnie shot back, looking now like he wanted to fight somebody.

"Whoa, whoa, whoa," I said, waving my hands. "Time out, guys. Let's just agree none of us know what's really out there—okay?" That got a much less than enthusiastic agreement to disagree from everyone. Although I was certain I heard Ronald mutter something like, *Not Rudy,* under his breath.

We had planned to camp out in the woods behind the neighborhood and adjacent to Two-Mile Swamp that night, but after Donnie's story, everyone, including myself, was having second thoughts. Well, everyone except Ronald, that is. He kept talking big, but in reality, I knew he had a deep-seated fear of the dark just like the rest of us. Together we were good, but put any one of us out in the woods alone with strange noises all around and we might just crap our pants.

"Okay," Donnie said, "say it's not true. If Buddy and Daniel know we're out here, they'll try to scare us anyway."

Donnie had a valid point. His brother would know what we were up to and would surely tell Buddy. Those two, along with a couple of the other older boys in the neighborhood, had terrorized us on many occasions. Being dark would make it ten times worse.

"I've got an idea," Toad said with a wry smile crossing his face. "What if we set the tent up at your house?" He looked at me. "After dark, we sneak out into the woods to settle this Rudy thing once and for all."

It was a good plan I thought, except for the Rudy part. If Buddy and Daniel thought we were at my house, they would never bother us there.

Good-natured fun was one thing, but when Buddy had pushed me down one day, he got a lot more than he bargained for. He was sixteen, and I was only nine at the time. After he pushed me, I went home crying.

22

It just so happened that my older brother was at the house. He asked me what was wrong. When I told him what had gone on, he insisted on following me back over to the wooded area where Buddy, Daniel, and a couple other older boys were hanging out smoking dope. When I stepped back through the bushes, Buddy got up and started at me, asking if I was back for more, but when my brother stepped out from behind me, Buddy stopped dead in his tracks with eyes as big as saucers. I don't think he had ever seen anyone that big before.

We had not lived in this area long, so very few kids outside of my friends had ever even seen my brother. He was nineteen at the time and strong from playing football and wrestling all throughout high school.

He stood six feet, two inches, and was every bit of 270 pounds, an imposing figure, to say the least. When he started at Buddy, the two older boys stood up and flocked to his side, but Daniel, not wanting any part of this, stayed put.

I wasn't certain what their strategy was at the time. Looking back, I guess they somehow thought three skinny dope heads might intimidate my brother since one obviously did not. Anyway, it did not work out in their favor. I had never seen three guys hit the ground so hard and so fast. Nor had I ever seen anyone over the age of twelve cry, plead, beg, and pee their pants like Buddy did. It was great!

Needless to say, I never had any trouble with those boys picking on me ever again, and as the story made its way around the neighborhood, nearly no one else bothered me either.

It was settled then. We were setting up camp in my backyard to throw off Buddy and Daniel, then about ten-thirty, we would sneak off into the woods to search for Rudy.

"Feel that?" asked Ronald, getting to his feet. The trestle was vibrating, signaling to us the train was coming. "Let's get out of here before we wind up dangling from the timbers again when it crosses."

We headed back to the neighborhood, gathered up supplies, and pitched the tent in the middle of my backyard late that afternoon. My mom had gotten us half a dozen bags of chips from the Oak Grove Superette and made a pile of sandwiches for us. She put them on ice in a Styrofoam cooler and mixed up a pitcher of root beer Kool-Aid to go with them.

No one other than me seems to remember the root beer flavor of Kool-Aid, but I loved it.

Planning on saving the sandwiches for later, the four of us pooled our change and headed off down the dirt road that led out of our neighborhood to get some candy at Taylor's Poultry Place. It was the closest thing to a convenience store in our neighborhood. Mostly, they just sold fresh-cut chicken, but they had a candy rack and drinks, too.

After that, we pretty much piddled around the rest of the day, deciding to conserve our energy for the planned expedition that night. It wouldn't get dark until around nine o'clock, after which, we would still have an hour and a half before we needed to leave. We figured that would be a good time to eat the sandwiches to get ready for the long hike down the tracks toward Two-Mile Swamp.

Somehow, we all managed to doze off in that tent. It was well past dark when I felt someone shaking me.

"Get up!" Ronald shouted at me.

"I'm awake," I shot back, trying to get the cobwebs out of my head. "What time is it?"

"I don't know," Ronald said, "but it's really dark out there, and we've got to get out of here."

He kicked Toad to wake him. Looking around the tent, we saw that Donnie was nowhere to be seen.

"Where's Donnie?" I asked.

"Don't know," Ronald said, shoving a sandwich in his mouth. "He was gone when I woke up."

"He must have chickened out," Toad said.

"Probably," Ronald agreed, "but we can't worry about that now. It's time to go!"

I wasn't too sure about this. It was scary enough when it was the four of us, but now only three? But no matter how hard we protested, it quickly became clear that no amount of trying was going to change Ronald's mind, so off we went.

The moon was already high by the time the three of us finally made our way down the long stretch of tracks deep into Two-Mile Swamp. Toad and I had tried several more times along the way to convince Ronald to turn around, but once we had crossed the Rutherford, putting that trestle behind us, there was no turning back. He was determined to prove, once and for all, that he was right and we were wrong.

From our vantage point atop the berm, we could see the blackish water glistening in the waning moonlight. We were roughly thirty feet or so above the swamp, but with the still, black water spread out below us, it gave the appearance we were much higher. If not for the moonlight, it would have been nearly impossible to tell where the water intersected the berm at all.

This was the midway point, as near as we could tell, and the deepest part of the swamp. Although I didn't really believe the old legend, my heart jumped up in my throat just a little when Toad directed the flashlight beam down the northside bank and spotted a swath of the old thorny brush that was much thinner than on either side. The area was about ten feet wide and looked as if there had been a path through it at some point.

"Give me a couple rocks!" Ronald called loudly at us from the opposite side of the tracks, startling Toad and me as we were still eyeing the bottom or the north side slope. We guessed it was at least fifty feet down to the briars, so that meant the swamp was twenty feet deep or more on the other side.

At Ronald's request, we had gathered a bunch of fist-sized rocks on the way over. We put them in an old burlap sack we had brought with us that my dad had tucked away in the garage. Honestly, Toad and I hadn't really questioned the reasoning behind it. I guess we figured they would come in handy to scare off wild animals or defend ourselves if necessary.

"Shhh!" was Toad's reply, spoken in a hushed tone as he crossed to the swamp side of the tracks. "You'll wake up Rudy — if there is such a thing!" He handed Ronald three rocks out of the sack.

"What do you think these are going to do?" Ronald asked, snickering, as he hurled one rock after another into the calm, black water. "Think they're going to wake up Rudy?"

"What the heck?" I said, squatting down quickly, still open to the absurd possibility the ghost of the murdered brakeman might just rise out of the murky water at any moment to exact his revenge on us. "You're going to get us killed!"

Ronald just laughed. "Killed by what?" he asked sarcastically. "Rudy?" He shook his head as he turned to look at us. "I'm telling you there's nothing that's going to hurt us in that swamp! Not even a 'gator!" he finished with a defiant tone.

It was pretty silly, I thought to myself as I remained squatting low to the graveled surface of the railroad berm. To think some *ghost* could haunt the middle of a swamp only to emerge on moonlit summer nights to prey upon anyone who happened into the swamp at midnight was pretty ridiculous when you thought about it. And I had been thinking a lot about it.

I guess Toad was thinking it, too, because at just about the same time we all started laughing—laughing hard. So hard, in fact, that I lost my balance when my foot caught on the track. I reeled back and fell on my butt. After seeing me sprawled out on the gravel surface, Ronald and Toad both dropped down where they were standing and roared with laughter, tears streaming down their faces.

This went on for several minutes, then Ronald yelled, "Stop!" quickly extinguishing the laughter.

"Do you feel that?" he asked, sitting on the ground with his palms planted firmly on the stony surface of the berm.

A low rumble gradually overtook the ground beneath us. We eased up off the berm and to our feet, standing perfectly still, all eyes gravitating toward the swamp. The calm, black water was suddenly rippling wildly and pulsating as the rumble grew more intense with every passing second. We remained quiet and motionless, staring intently at the now almost roiling water, as bits of gravel and the earthen berm dislodged beneath our feet. The material cascaded down the steep slope, making an eerie, plunking sound as it made contact with the water.

Ronald and Toad got to their feet on the swamp side of the tracks and retreated back to the safety of rail line as I, still on the north side, got up and started toward the rails myself.

Seemingly out of nowhere, a burst of light flooded over us and the swamp, as two-hundred tons of steel rounded the bend, screaming toward us at seventy miles per hour. The blinding light and deafening howl of the train whistle disoriented Ronald and Toad, who now stood dead in the center of the tracks.

With only seconds to spare, I lunged myself at my friends, shoving them hard off the tracks, twisting my body just in time to roll out of the speeding train's path. Falling face-first, I hit the gravel surface with a solid thud. Quickly pushing up on my palms, I looked under the train to the opposite side of the tracks and saw Ronald and Toad lying on the gravel as the train passed between us. With very little room between the speeding train and the steep slope, they lay clinging to the stony surface, fighting to keep from sliding down into the swamp.

Ronald lay prone, parallel to the tracks, with his head turned to face me. His pained expression and streaming tears told me he was either hurt, scared, or both. Toad lay just beyond him with half his body dangling over the slope. He looked straight ahead, digging his chin into the graveled surface and clawing desperately at the loose rocks. I tried calling out to them to hang on, but the rhythmic din of the train wheels racing past drowned out any and all other sounds.

Looking past Ronald and Toad, I caught sight of an eerie, growing red luminosity emanating from the swamp. The shimmering crimson aura crept up the embankment and slowly slithered over Toad as its source neared the edge of the slope. The light washed over Toad's eyes, and a terrified look gripped his face. He burst into tears and tried to scream, but the screeching train drowned out the sound of his voice.

The dim red glow spread through the under-carriage of the train as the rapidly passing wheels created momentary gaps in my field of vision, reminiscent of the flickering of an early silent projection film. Then, in the blink of an eye—Toad was gone.

Ronald, having seen the horrified expression on my face, turned to look in Toad's direction. Seeing no sign of him, Ronald pushed himself up on his hands and knees. He crawled toward the edge. He stopped dead, then slowly rose to his feet. All I could see were his feet as he calmly stepped toward the embankment.

Suddenly, from the left, a dark figure barreled into Ronald, and they both hit the ground hard. I saw Ronald lying face-down in the gravel as the figure straddled him on his knees and turned Ronald's head back in my direction, away from the swamp. Then, after springing back to its feet, the dark figure quickly leapt over the embankment.

As I locked eyes with Ronald once more, I saw that his expression had transformed into one of shock and sheer terror. What had he seen in the swamp? Out of nowhere, to Ronald's left, a powerful arm thrust up from below and dug its fingers deep into the gravel bed as the last train car passed.

Bounding to my feet, I darted across the tracks to Ronald's side, intent on grabbing him and getting us out of there.

"Give me a hand!" came a familiar-sounding voice from the embankment, "but don't look into the swamp!"

The voice was Buddy's. The arm flung over the top of the berm was his. With his back pressed hard against the slope, heels dug into the steep bank, Buddy inched his way up the embankment, dragging Toad behind him.

Heeding Buddy's warning not to look into the swamp, I knelt down, gripped the warm train rail with my left hand for support, reached over with my right hand, but hesitated.

"How do I know I can trust you, that this isn't just another scheme you and Daniel cooked up to scare us?"

"Look, there's no time for this crap. I'll be fine, but if I have to let go, Herbie boy here's a goner!"

And with that, I hesitantly offered my hand to Buddy. The dim red glow seemed to have retreated a bit, but the tiny amount of light that caught my eye calmed me somehow, and I felt my grip on the rail relaxing.   Buddy, noticing the shift in my body, yelled up at me, "Look away!" His shout jolted me out of my daze, but not before my hand slipped off the rail and sent Buddy and Toad sliding perilously back down the slope.

Now Buddy was just out of my reach. I frantically scanned the top of the berm for something to use to pull him up. I spotted the burlap sack of rocks lying on the tracks and quickly snatched it up. Clenching the top of the sack with my right hand, I tossed the weighted end over the edge to Buddy and again grabbed the rail.

I shut my eyes tight to shield myself from the red glow and felt Buddy tug on the sack. It took every ounce of strength I had to get him over the berm's edge where together we were able to drag Toad to the top of the berm.

"Is he dead?" I asked, opening my eyes to look at Toad.

"No," Buddy said calmly, feeling Toad's neck for a pulse, "I got to him in time."

Exhausted, we sat back against the rail, and Buddy looked down into the swamp.

"How'd you know where to find us?" I asked.

"Donnie," he said, "I was at his house when he tried to sneak past me and Daniel. We started giving him crap about being afraid of the dark and leaving you guys to fend for yourselves in that tent. He went along with it for a bit, then 'fessed up that he was scared because you guys were going looking for Rudy. I had no choice at that point. I told them I had to go and headed out here to find you guys."

"But how'd you know about Rudy?" I asked, grateful that he had come.

"That's a long story," Buddy said, apparently not wanting or willing to elaborate. "Go ahead, look if you want to," he said to me. "Just turn your head away quickly. Understand?"

"But you said not to look," I replied.

"He can't hurt you while I'm here," Buddy said, "and this may be your only chance to see him."

Unsure that I wanted to see whatever was in the swamp, I reluctantly turned my head anyway. Then I saw it—a bloated, grotesque shimmering figure of a man floating ankle-deep in the water. His slimy, tattered clothing was rooted with thin, stringy vines that intertwined and meandered through his translucent gray corpse-like skin and sunken, hollow eyes. A mangled jaw framed his toothless, frothing mouth. Spindly arms with rotted flesh showed through the shredded remains of his coat and ended in long, bony, skinless fingers. I was horrified.

The ghostly apparition shifted his weight repeatedly on legs that rocked back and forth where he stood. His head cocked from side to side, rolling and bobbling violently. Deep, guttural sounds rose from his throat as if he were trying to communicate but couldn't.

In his right hand, he clutched a brakeman's lantern, the source of the red glow. As my eyes fell upon it, the strange calm overwhelmed me again, and I felt compelled to walk toward the light

As I began to rise, Buddy raked an arm across me and barked, "Look away!" again, breaking my daze. "That's how he gets you. The light from the lantern somehow draws you to him. He can't hurt you unless you enter the swamp."

"Why doesn't it affect you?" I asked Buddy.

He smiled grimly, shook his head, and forced out a nervous laugh under his breath. "I think it's the color of light coming from the lantern," he said

"You mean the red?" I asked, not understanding.

"Red?" Buddy repeated and nodded at me. "So that's what color it is. I could never tell because I'm color blind."

"Let's get these guys up and back to the tent," Buddy said as we pulled Ronald and Toad to their feet.

As we started back down the tracks, I could not help but glance back over my shoulder one last time. As revolting a sight as Rudy was, I knew his story, and I felt deeply sorry for him. But try as I might, I could not relate to the unimaginable loneliness and feeling of loss he must have experienced all these years.

With his lantern now submerged, I watched Rudy slowly dissolve back into the swamp. For the briefest of moments, I saw a spark of life pour back into his hollow eyes as his thin, decaying lips seemed to form a single word.

Please.

DEAN'S MACHINE

I HAD TRAVELED the narrow winding trail through the thick pine forest bordering Two-Mile Swamp many times before that day and never noticed the shiny twisted steel and tire carcass just off the well-worn path. Veined with thin, wiry vines, it appeared the mangled wreckage had been there for quite a while. Except that other than the glaring physical damage, its contorted remains showed little wear. The shiny silver paint glistened when struck by the narrow beams of sunlight that pierced the thick overhead canopy.

It was the light reflecting off the wreck's shimmering surface that first caught my attention, or at least I had thought it was. These were dense woods, thick with underbrush and briars. Even more so the closer you got to the swamp. I rarely, if ever before that day, ventured off the trail—especially when I was alone.

The plan to meet my friends—Ronald, Donnie, and Toad—after lunch and hike the trail together had gone awry when my mother insisted, "Richard, do your chores before you leave the house."

That made me late, and the guys had gone on without me. I was the youngest of the group, having turned eleven at the beginning of the summer. Donnie and Toad were both teenagers, a year ahead of Ronald in school, and two years ahead of me. But even at eleven I was almost six-feet tall and bigger than any of them.

Toad was a nickname Ronald had hung on Herbert after he licked a toad, convinced it would make him high. He liked it, so the name stuck. We always picked at each other. In many ways we were more like brothers, I think. No matter what we got into, if there was trouble for one, there was trouble for all.

We had planned to go to our secret hangout, the small abandoned farmhouse we had discovered nestled deep in the woods at the beginning of the summer.

The four of us stumbled on the place by accident following strange screaming noises we had heard coming from farther in the woods. The farm, as it turned out, was situated behind a meat-packing plant, and the screaming we heard were the squeals of pigs being electrocuted to death before they were butchered.

The house, barn, and a few old broken hardwood trees stood in the center of a huge, fenced grassy field that spread out in all directions with a small herd of cattle milling about grazing. I imagined it had once been a family farm either for the packing plant's owners themselves, or some other family. The long abandoned shack of a house was little more than a shell of a structure that now teetered precariously on aged and broken red brick pilasters.

Rotted doors barely clung to rusted hinges, and shattered glass lay strewn throughout the home from windows destroyed by vandals and time. The wood-plank living room floor was partially collapsed and bore the scars of hoof prints from cows that at some point had roamed through the building. Now the former homestead sat ringed in yellow caution tape meant to deter anyone from entering — but it didn't.

Nearby, a large wooden barn stood tall, its left side facing the front of the house. Huge double-hung alley doors at each end were locked tight, bound by thick rust-coated chains looped through steel handles and padlocked. The open loft doors pivoted on weathered hinges that squeaked occasionally when coaxed by a gentle breeze, revealing bales of hay packed tightly from one end to the other. The worn graying wood siding, much of it split and broken, had flecks of red clinging to it in spots that looked more like a spattering of blood than paint. A rusty tin roof protected the barn's contents from the weather, mostly, except where a corner here and there had broken free of the nails and flapped occasionally when the wind gusted.

Along the side of the barn facing the house two small barbed-wire fenced pens extended. One held a great big spotted pig, a trough full of feed, and a mud hole for him to wallow in. He seemed friendly enough, but we had heard a pig could bite off a human hand, so we never tried to pet or hand-feed it.

The other pen held a dozen or so small goats at any given time. They were skittish, mean little creatures prone to biting and butting so we left them alone — for the most part.

Since discovering the farm, we had met daily at the trailhead and hiked back to hop the fence and cross the pasture to the old shack or loft, treating them like our clubhouse. The first few days we had gone early in the morning but ended up hiding in the loft when a couple of farmhands showed up to feed the pig and goats. That wasn't too bad at first. It became sort of a challenge to stay hidden from the men. The squeals of the dying pigs sounded more often during the mornings. When, on the third day, two men loaded up the big spotted pig and hauled it away, we decided not to come until the afternoons. It was quieter then.

The loft was easily accessible by a ladder at the back of the barn, and we spent plenty of time up there crawling over the bales and drinking in the smell of the fresh-cut hay. We told stories, played hide-and-seek, and dared each other to jump in the goat pen and try to get close enough to touch one without getting kicked or butted. But we never got into the barn itself though we tried.

Both ends were locked up tight, as was the trap-door from the loft. We often peered through the loft floorboards, or cracked gray wood siding, into the dimly lit barn. There was something in there, in the middle of the dirt floor, surrounded by bales of hay, with a large white tarp draped over it.

My thoughts drifted back to the moment and the shimmering vehicle before me when I heard the guys up ahead hooting and hollering. I yelled to them but apparently they were being too loud to hear my attempt to get their attention. Knowing I was near the farm, I decided, against my better judgment, to check out the wreckage.

The closer I got to this oddly intriguing car the more drawn and fascinated I was by it. How had it come to be so deep in these woods, and why hadn't I, or any of the guys, noticed it before? More than that, I could not grasp why it was not a rusted heap. As I circled it, I let my finger trace along the smooth undamaged portions of the body and noticed the flattened tires were still slick and black, crumpled steel's silver paint gleamed like new in the light, and the tattered and torn upholstery was a clean, rich red color. Even what remained of the shattered glass and mirrors was crystal clear.

"She's a beaut, ain't she?" came the unexpected voice from behind me, nearly causing me to jump out of my skin. I whirled to see who had snuck up on me, half expecting it to be Ronald or one of the guys trying to scare the wits out of me — but it wasn't.

"Sorry, kid, didn't mean to startle ya," the young man said with a chuckle, a wry smile pursing his lips as he strode toward the car.

I had thought the wreck looked out of place here, but when compared to the stranger standing before me, it looked almost normal. The man was in his early twenties with slicked-back dirty blond hair and deep blue eyes. His gruff voice did not fit his small frame, maybe five feet, eight inches and a hundred and forty pounds if he were soaking wet. He wore dark blue jeans that were cuffed at the ankle, a white short-sleeve T-shirt with the sleeves rolled up and a pack of cigarettes twisted up in the left sleeve. He had a swagger to him, and beamed a confidence much larger than he was. Aside from his diminutive stature, everything about this guy gave me the impression he was someone you wanted on your side, the kind of guy that would have your back in a fight, and not someone to be taken lightly. The man pulled the cigarettes from his sleeve revealing a pack of Lucky Strikes, and with a snap of his wrist, an unfiltered cigarette popped partially from the small torn opening and he offered it to me. I declined.

"Good man," he said with a nod, and in one fluid motion the stranger swept the pack across his mouth, pulled the cigarette out with his lips, and returned the Luckies to his sleeve. Then he reached into his right front pocket and dug out a heavy metal flip-top lighter and struck it several times before the flame came to life and he lit the cigarette. With a jerk of his wrist he snapped the lighter's top down and slid it back into his pocket.

He even did that with a swagger, I thought to myself as much in awe as fearful of this unusual little man.

The cigarette hung loosely, coolly, from his lips as he pulled a clean white rag from his rear pocket and went about carefully wiping down the car. I watched, uncertain what, if anything, to say to him as he moved about the car, almost lovingly, wiping every inch, avoiding only the damaged areas. He spoke aloud, not necessarily to me, as he spat into the cloth regularly, shined tires, glass, and mirrors, and buffed the shiny silver paint and the big black number *130* emblazoned on the hood and doors.

"This your car, mister?" I finally managed to blurt, certain it had to be, but not sure how else to spark a conversation.

"Yep, she's all mine," the stranger said, continuing to wipe down the car. "Only driven her a couple of times, though," he said in a lamenting tone. "I really need to take her out more often."

I was dumbfounded. Were we seeing the same car? He was talking about it like it was a running vehicle and not the twisted vine-enshrined heap I saw.

The aura around the car changed as he went on wiping, cleaning, and talking about it. I had felt drawn to the vehicle when I first saw it, but as he continued I became mesmerized by this man, his adoration toward the car — and the car itself.

"You want to go for a spin?" he asked beaming with pride. "This machine really wails on the open road!"

His invitation was ridiculous. I knew it, but still I felt compelled to get in the car, in the relatively intact passenger's side seat. As I moved closer, fear and apprehension gave way to curiosity, and I began to see the car the way the stranger must have.

Flattened tires rose as they filled with air. Contorted steel body parts smoothed as shiny silver paint flowed over them. Shattered and broken glass rippled like a gentle breeze across still water and became whole once more. And the tattered upholstery wove itself back together before my very eyes, renewing the rich red leather seats to their original beauty. In a matter of moments the wreck was completely transformed. Seeing it now, as the stranger surely had all along, I finally understood. The machine was beautiful.

The fellow slid into the driver's seat and turned over the ignition. The car purred to life. He revved the engine a few times and motioned for me to get in. The smooth sound of the motor was like a Siren's song — a call I could not resist. I started toward the passenger's side of the car, yet there was something, something else, some other nagging sound that caught my ear.

Richard, I heard someone say, the sound of my name half falling on my ears and in my head. I looked at the stranger curiously as he urged me to get in the car — to take a ride with him. *I hadn't told him my name.* The whole thing was unbelievable. "How do you know my name," I mouthed.

"Hey, Richard!" Ronald hollered from behind me, "you coming or not?"

I spun to look in his direction and almost lost my balance.

"We've been waiting for you at the fence," Ronald said, a touch of annoyance in his tone.

"I was," I started, stammering, "getting ready to go for a ride." I finished under my breath turning back toward the suddenly silent car — it was gone.

"What was that?" Ronald asked, obviously confused by what he thought he had just heard me say.

"Nothing," I said shaking my head, staring at the empty thicket where the car, and the stranger, had been just seconds earlier, "nothing at all."

"How long have you guys been waiting for me?" I asked Ronald.

"It's been a while," he said. "We've already been up to the barn but when we saw it was gone, we ran back down to come find you."

"Saw what was gone?" I asked reaching out to snatch Ronald by the shoulder and turn him toward me.

"Whatever was in the barn," he said with a smile. "It's gone."

"So the barn doors are open?" I asked still reeling from my experience.

"No," he said, "that's the weird part. It's all locked up like it was before. Hay bales haven't moved either, but that white tarp thingy is just laying flat on the ground." Ronald turned and ran to the fence where Donnie and Toad stood waving me on.

I watched him run to the metal fence with its two barbwire strands that made up the last foot at the top and climb over it. The sensation crept over me once again that something was luring me back. I started to turn when a small rock struck me in the forehead.

"Ouch!" I hollered reaching up to rub the spot where it hit me. Across the fence stood a satisfied-looking Ronald rearing back to fire another one. I went after him like a rocket.

My experience that day, the stranger with a swagger like none other I had met before or since, and the car would haunt me for some time. Was it real, a daydream, an illusion—or a ghost? All questions I struggled with for many years, but I never walked those trails alone again.

Thirty-eight years have passed since that summer day. As an adult, I have taken up paranormal research as a hobby, attending well-organized conventions with authorities who speak about the supernatural. It was during one of those mass events, when the lights lowered, that grainy black and white images projected on a large screen shed some light on that eerie event from so long ago.

As the speaker began his talk, I saw the familiar swagger of the stranger from my memory flash up before my eyes. He stood proudly beside a shiny silvery car with a big black *130* emblazoned on the hood and doors. The car was a 1955 Porsche 550 Spyder, and the stranger, James Dean, had died in that car twenty-two years before I saw them.

James Dean was before my time, but the speaker explained, "Dean's brief stint in Hollywood forever etched his memory among the greatest actors of his day—and beyond. By today's standards you would liken him to Tom Cruise if he had been struck down just after *Top Gun*, or to Leonardo DiCaprio, had he died horrifically after *Titanic*."

The speaker went on to explain the legend of Dean's car. It sounded like the plot of a Hollywood horror film. According to the presenter, shortly after getting the car, Dean showed the Spyder to his friend, Alec Guinness, who told Dean he felt that the car was cursed, and that if Dean drove it, he would be dead in a week. Seven days later Dean was killed in a head-on collision while driving the Porsche.

"Two men who later salvaged parts from the wrecked Porsche were subsequently killed in separate accidents the first time they drove their cars using the salvaged parts from James Dean's car," the man said.

"The Spyder, in its wrecked form, traveled the country being displayed at high schools as a deterrent to speeding." The speaker paused for effect. "When unusual occurrences and accidents became associated with the car's presence at every stop, authorities halted the tour, and sent the car to a warehouse for storage.

"That building burned to the ground the very first night Dean's car was there. The Porsche was the only thing to survive the fire. When the wreckage was next transported, the flat-bed truck carrying the vehicle overturned and its driver was killed. Dean's car landed on him when he was thrown from the truck."

The audience gasped, but the story continued. "The last time anyone laid eyes on the Spyder was when it was loaded into a truck and shipped from the East Coast across the country to California. But when the driver arrived at his destination, Dean's car had disappeared from the locked trailer without a trace — and without an explanation."

The speaker let that settle in to the hushed crowd, then went on to explain that for decades after the car's unexplained disappearance, sightings of a strange young man and the shiny silver twisted remains were being reported all along the path Dean's car was reported to have traveled on its final journey across the country.

Some witnesses declared they had seen only the car, while others claimed to have seen a young man with the wreck. Some saw neither the car nor the man, stating only that they had heard the sound of a finely tuned car engine fading into the distance just before a friend or loved one disappeared. But no one had ever described seeing the Porsche 550 Spyder restored — or being offered a ride in it.

Not until I raised my hand . . .

WHISPERING PINES

OLD MATHIAS called them Grand Pines. Not loblolly, longleaf, or white pines, which were common in the South, but Grand Pines with capital letters. He claimed they were the only two left standing anywhere in the world, and that he was the one who had planted them as saplings centuries ago.

Mathias Whetstone was the first black man I ever met. My father moved us from Pennsylvania to South Carolina in 1975, just after my second-grade year. Where I was raised until then, in the small township of Milford, there just were not any black people.

Mathias was a puny little man with thick white curly hair that was yellowed at the ends. Small round ears on either side of his head swept forward giving him an almost cartoonish look. His nearly black, dark brown eyes showed languid through the milky haze that gathers with age. He was much darker-skinned than any black man I had seen on television, or in the movies, with a wrinkled face coarsely etched by time.

Mathias had scared the dickens out of us the first time he popped up out of nowhere on one of our romps through Two-Mile Swamp. He told us he lived in the swamp, though none of us ever saw his home. And we had been all over that place. Later, we would run across him from time to time whenever we dared to venture really, really deep into the swamp. I should say we never actually found him. More like he would find us, but we almost always knew if he was around because of the sweet smell of pipe tobacco wafting on the otherwise musky swamp air.

There were three things old Mathias was never without—his corncob pipe, a bright cheery smile, and a story. We would sit for hours and listen to his tales, some from centuries past about the Gloo Loo Indian tribe that once claimed the area that would become Two-Mile Swamp as their own. Legends of strange terrifying creatures that roamed the surrounding lands by night. And all the unexplained disappearances and happenings that have occurred since the last of the Gloo Loo tribe were slaughtered in the mid 1800s.

Most of Mathias' stories were meant to entertain us, and that they did. But others served to warn us to stay away from certain areas of the swamp, especially during the full moon.

Donnie, Toad, and I always took heed of the old man's warnings while Ronald thought it was all bunk. He respected old-man Mathias enough not to say it to his face, but he had no problem declaring it to us.

"That old man is full of crap! Creatures in the swamp, Indian burial mounds, Voodoo, mysterious lights, come on—you guys aren't really buying all that garbage, are you?" Ronald asked, shaking his head.

"They're good stories," I shot back at him, "whether they're true or not doesn't matter. Why do you always have to ruin it for the rest of us?"

"Not everything in this here swamp is dangerous." The voice that came from behind us had a hint of squeakiness with the telltale tremble of a very old man.

None of us had any idea this time that Mathias was near. Ronald turned beet red with embarrassment realizing that the old man had heard his rant.

"I'm sorry, Mr. Matthias," Ronald said, his head hung low. "I didn't mean no disrespect."

"None taken, boy," Mathias said as he emerged from the wood line stuffing his corncob pipe full of tobacco. "Like you was sayin', they ain't nothin' but stories until you actually experience them for yourself. Ain't that right?" He eyed Ronald, Toad, and me.

"Yes, sir." Ronald said with a nod, the red fading as his embarrassment eased.

"That's why I'm going to take you boys to see somethin' that ain't gonna hurt you, and that no one other than me has ever seen — The Grand Pines."

Intrigued, we followed Mathias deeper than we had ever gone into the swamp. The sweet smell of his pipe tickled our nostrils as the old man told us the legend of the Grand Pines — and *how* special these last two were — but not *why*. He moved deftly through heavy briar-laden brush as if following a path unseen to us, but clearly visible to him. While the four of us spat a chorus of *yikes* and *ouches*, or worse in Ronald's case, as sharp barbs tore at our clothes and exposed skin.

All was forgotten when we stepped through a hedge of tightly intertwined scrub oaks and into a huge circular clearing slap dab in the middle of the swamp. The opening had to be the size of a football field across. Nearly a perfect circle ringed completely by the scrub oaks. A swath of loamy detritus formed from years of cast-off leaves and sticks from the oaks, and long finger-thick pine needles and barrel-sized pine cones smashed into the ring of debris followed the arc of the dense tree line to either side of the spot where we had emerged.

"That's a dang meteorite," Ronald said, staring blankly ahead.

In the center of all of this, surrounded by a moat of soupy green luminescent water, a huge black, pitted rock marbled with veins of what looked like quartz rose above the eerie glowing muck. Upon that stood the two biggest trees any of us had ever seen.

They were the pine tree equivalent of redwoods. The two enormous trunks sprang from the rocky mound only an arm's length apart at the bottom, then angled away from one another as they towered toward the heavens.

"Meteor," Donnie corrected.

"Huh?" Ronald said, shooting a sideways glance at Donnie.

"Meteorites are in space," Donnie said with just a hint of awe in his tone. "Once they've hit the ground, they're meteors."

There was a shared understanding as the rest of us nodded.

Toad, dumbfounded, absently wandered toward the edge of a narrow patch of soft earth between us and the swampy moat encircling the trees. He was trying to see the tops which were shrouded by fog or mist—maybe even clouds as tall as these trees were.

"Richard, grab him!" someone hollered at me. Donnie, I think, startling me out of my own giant-tree induced malaise. I caught sight of Toad, already one foot hovering over the edge, just in time to snatch him back by the collar of his shirt.

The sudden movement rocked him back and off his feet, and he plopped to the ground, landing solidly on his butt. "Ouch!" he exclaimed, vigorously rubbing the injured area. "Not on my tailbone again. This thing's never going to heal."

Seeing Toad's comically pained expression got a belly laugh out of Ronald. And for just a moment we all joined in. Fueled more by Ronald's barking laughter than poor Toad's broken coccyx.

"What y'all find funny 'bout that?" Mathias asked earnestly as he helped Toad to his feet. "That boy's tailbone would've been the least of his worries had he stepped into that there moat." He pointed at the green water.

We were quiet as we looked from the old man to the moat, then back at one another.

"But you said it wasn't dangerous," Ronald tried to argue.

"I *said*," Mathias started, putting the emphasis on the word said, pointing at the rocky island. "That them trees isn't dangerous."

Ronald eyed the moat warily, then looked back to Mathias.

"There's things that live in that there water, boy. That water what made them trees grow big as they are," Mathias said sweeping one frail bony hand up toward the sky.

We all stepped back from the edge as far as we could. Even Toad, who could be a little dense, had understood the old man's implication. "Maybe we should go?" I suggested, which was quickly followed by a silent chorus of bobbing heads nodding their approval.

As if on cue, the water roiled. Suspended vegetation, algae, and yellowish froth that drifted sparsely on the luminescent surface parted. A pair of basketball eyes on a triangular head slowly broke the surface and peered at Toad.

"Not so fast, boys," Mathias said, seemingly unfazed by the creature's sudden appearance. "I haven't told you what's so special about these here trees," he finished, showing his few yellow teeth in a wide grin.

"Well," Ronald started, "let's see." His tone was as sarcastic as it was tinged with anxiety. He swept both hands toward the pines in an exaggerated motion. "They're gargantuan, and drop needles and cones that could kill a man." Ronald pointed at the base of the trees. "They appear to have sprouted out of a meteor, which we all know from science fiction movies and comic books can't be good." He sucked in a quick breath. "Oh, and there's the green glowing pool that contains at least one Godzilla-sized alligator." Ronald rested his hands on his knees sucking in gulps of air in rapid succession, but managed to blurt one last statement. "But you haven't *told* us. What's so special?"

Donnie walked over to Ronald who was on the verge of hyperventilating. Toad and I stood frozen and looked from Ronald to Mathias. The old man's expression had changed just barely. He still had the same gap-toothed grin splayed across his coarse face as he eyed Ronald. Behind those dark eyes, there was a hint of concern showing as he watched Donnie guide Ronald through a series of breathing exercises to help calm him.

It took maybe a minute for us to realize the only sounds we were hearing, besides Ronald's subsiding labored breaths, was a faint unintelligible whisper emanating from the trees. Toad and I turned toward the pines at the same time. Ronald and Donnie were almost immediately at our side, and we just stared.

The lines of crisscrossing quartz had begun to sparkle and glow. The light that emanated bathed the meteor and the base of the trees, in an orb of white light.

Mathias strolled past us headed toward the moat. I started to reach for him, thinking he was about to fall victim to the gatorsaurus, but the creature, its gaze fixed on the tiny old man, slowly retreated into the depths as Mathias approached.

The old man stopped abruptly at water's edge. He spun with purpose to look at us, spreading his arms out to either side. Then he threw back his head and bellowed in a clear loud voice reminiscent of a carnival barker, "I give you the Whispering Pines."

Mathias' voice boomed, casting an echo that reverberated all around us that gradually died and was replaced by a crescendo of whispers — the whispers and another sound. Subtler, more natural, but too frequent. Cracking and popping mixed with a dragging — no, a slithering noise.

"Guys," Donnie called, a tremor in his voice, "look!" We turned to see what had drawn his attention and saw the ring of scrub oaks intertwining their branches into an impenetrable wall of thatch. Huge luminescent green vines, the color of the moat water, wove their way horizontally through and around the wall of trees. Each sprouted tiny fingers that spread perpendicular, up and down, until the entire structure was an iridescent wall of shimmering shades of green.

Donnie rushed at the wall, but Ronald tackled him to the ground. "What the heck, Ronald?" Donnie stammered. "We've got to get through that wall!" He struggled to get up, but Ronald fought to hold him down.

"Look at it!" Ronald screamed in Donnie's face. "It's probably radioactive. Maybe even gamma rays."

That quieted Donnie. He sat up quickly and stared at the wall. What we knew about gamma radiation was garnered from Marvel Comics' *The Incredible Hulk* comic book. We had already guessed the strange rock formation was most likely a meteor. In nearly every science fiction monster movie I'd ever seen, a radioactive meteor was the cause of some monster or another.

As we pondered that, a new sound elevated itself above the whispers. We turned to see the circular patch of detritus inside the tree wall being sucked away by turbulent moat waters. Eyes again appeared from below, rising above the glowing, roiling waters. Not just a single pair, but multiple sets of eyes broke the surface.

The four of us huddled together as close to the illuminated wall as we could without touching it. A wave of heat at our backs reinforced Ronald's theory. Mathias stood his ground at the moat edge, unmoved by what was happening around him.

As rapidly as the material was whisked away from the tree line, it reappeared, coalescing into a narrow bridge-like walkway that formed quickly, extending from just behind where the old man stood toward the trees. Once the bridge had connected the twenty-foot semicircle of debris that remained where we stood, the deterioration of the path ended. The disturbance in the moat abruptly calmed, the sound of sloshing waters dying as the whispering intensified.

We cautiously broke our huddle and eyed the narrow bridge, acutely aware that six pairs of eyes, three on either side of the earthen walkway, and each attached to the head of a gatorsaurus, watched us intently.

"Who's first?" Mathias barked in an upbeat tone, again displaying what few teeth he had in a cheerful grin.

We exchanged a few looks with one another, but no one said a word. The apprehension—no, that's an understatement. The fear in each other's eyes was palpable. We were still processing all this when Mathias cleared his throat loudly.

"There's no turnin' back now, boys. One of you has gots to go across that bridge," he said, his tone a bit more stern than I had ever heard him speak to us before.

"You go!" Ronald blurted with anger seeping into the tremor of fear in his tone.

Mathias' grin melted, and he eyed Ronald sternly. "Don't take that tone with me, boy!" the old man spat, suddenly nose-to-nose with Ronald after closing the gap between them so fast we barely saw him move.

Ronald's eyes went wide. He put up his hands defensively and stepped back, stopping when he felt the burn from the wall beneath his clothes. "I don't understand what's happening," he said, tears forming in his eyes, and more fear in his voice than I had ever heard.

Mathias' grin returned, and I saw compassion in his expression. He put a hand on Ronald's shoulder. He flinched at the old man's touch. "I apologize, boy. That's my fault. Let me explain it to you." He removed his hand and walked toward the bridge.

"Ya'll listen up, now," he said in an authoritative tone. "You hear those whispers, don't you?" Mathias turned his gaze toward us. We all nodded at him. He swept one thin hand toward the trees. "That's those pines talkin' to us. That's why I calls them the Whispering Pines."

The tenor of whispers rose and fell as Mathias spoke. Never too loud, or too soft. Mostly unintelligible except for an occasional word—or name.

"Ronald."

We all heard the Pines say his name. Ronald froze at that, and Mathias stared at him.

"I—I—I," Ronald stammered. His breathing began to labor again. Donnie walked to his side. Ronald continued, "I don't understand what they're saying."

"You ain't gonna, boy. Less you get right up between them trees," Mathias said, pointing at the gap between the pines. "You know what them whispers is?" the old man asked eyeing the four of us again.

We exchanged quick glances, then shook our heads in unison.

"Them's *secrets*!" he said ardently. "Knowledge. Those trees will tell you things no one else knows."

Ronald scrunched up his face in thought. Toad chimed in before he could speak. "Like where to find buried treasure?"

"Maybe," the old man said with a nod.

"If Atlantis is real?" Donnie piped up enthusiastically. The old man shrugged.

"Maybe they'll tell me where Jimmy Hoffa is buried," Ronald said smugly. Mathias frowned. Donnie popped Ronald in the back of the head.

"Ouch!"

"It don't exactly work like that," Mathias said. "You don't get to ask no questions. The trees just tell you what they want to."

"What good is that?" Ronald asked. "Maybe it's something I don't want to know, or don't care about."

"Then you keeps it to yourself, boy," Mathias said. "No matter whats, you keep it to yourself."

"What good is a secret you can't do anything with?" I asked.

"Didn't say you couldn't act on it. Just can't tells nobody." Mathias scolded.

"Oh," I said.

"So, who's going first?" the old man asked and then looked at Ronald. "They's been calling your name, boy."

Ronald eyed the narrow walkway. It was three-feet wide at best, and rose out of the moat about two feet. The gatorsauruses on each side had drifted closer to the pathway. Two had just tangled with one another for a brief moment as one attempted to nudge the other out of the way.

"Heck, no!" Ronald barked. "Those things will eat me."

Mathias let out a hearty laugh. "Them little ole gators?" he mused. "They can't come outs the water or touch the land. As long as you stay on the path, they ain't gonna eat you."

Little ole gators, I thought to myself. Was he seeing the same thing we were?

Ronald hesitated and I spoke up. "Only one of us needs to go—then we can leave, right?" Mathia nodded once.

"Then I'll go," I said and started toward the bridge.

"Wait a darn minute," Ronald said, stepping forward to cut me off. "Those trees have been calling *my* name. Maybe it's something I'm supposed to know." He paused, then turned to Mathias. "I'll go."

Mathias' wide grin parted his face and he made a shooing motion toward Ronald.

Ronald eased onto the raised pathway. One of the giant gators sidled up next to where he stood. He had walked about twenty-feet when the creature opened its huge jaws, then snapped them shut on the water. Green murky water splashed, showering Ronald with tiny droplets. He screamed. Then the gator thrashed, sending torrents of water into the air. Waves crashed against Ronald. His feet went out from under him and he nearly tumbled into the moat on the opposite side of the monster and into the open maw of another of the great beasts. The other four shot toward the frenzy and began thrashing and splashing.

"Run!" I hollered as loud as I could over the cacophony of sounds that was emphasized by the roar of the huge creatures. Toad and Donnie yelled, also. Almost as loud as us was Mathias' laughter.

Ronald sprang to his feet and bolted for the trees. He'd caught the monsters off-guard. They had all congregated together where Ronald had nearly fallen off the path. When he bolted, their huge bodies collided with each other, and Ronald easily crossed the hundred-feet or so to the island.

"Take that!" Ronald screamed at the gargantuan gators as he threw a chunk of rock that struck one solidly between its eyes. "You didn't tell me about that, old man," he yelled defiantly at Mathias.

"You didn't ask," the old man quipped with a chuckle.

Toad, Donnie, and I moved away from Mathias. He shot us a sideways glance and shook his head.

The whispers suddenly pitched higher again, and the gators submerged. The only other audible sound was the disturbance of the moat waters as ripples spread out and licked at the raised pathway.

A flicker of recognition washed over Ronald's face, and he turned toward the trees. We watched him climb the black rock to where the two Grand Pines stood and position himself between them. There was a change in the light as Ronald lowered his head and listened. The glowing sphere of luminescence pulsed in sync with the whispers which came more rapidly now. Ronald's face contorted as he cocked his head slightly as if straining to hear, or understand, something that was either spoken too softly, or too quickly, or in an accent that required the listener to concentrate.

Then it stopped. The volume of the whispers dropped. The orb dimmed and the pulsing vanished. Ronald looked up. His face was a mix of confusion and disgust as he stepped forward and threw up his hands to cup his mouth.

Out of the corner of my eye, I saw Mathias' chin drop to his chest. The old man shook his head slowly and deliberately, and I realized he knew what Ronald was about to do. I sprang forward and started to yell — but it was too late.

"Any of you guys ever heard of Timmy Hall?" Ronald bellowed at us. He'd barely gotten the name out of his mouth when a bolt of pure white energy erupted from the ground. It arced from one Grand Pine to the other, passing straight through Ronald as it completed the circuit. Ronald screamed as his body seized into a fetal position and dropped. The white energy crackled and sizzled as the arc continued up, rising between the two enormous trees until it fizzled with a flash and loud pop somewhere in the haziness that shrouded the tops of the trees from our view.

Ronald's body abruptly released itself from the forced fetal position. He tumbled down the rock to land flat on his face on the narrow path. One languid arm flopped over the edge and into the water.

Almost immediately huge eyes and triangular heads breached the smooth moat waters, and the whispers rose again in volume.

"Richard."

Mathias flinched just as I heard my name. I thought I saw the old man start to move in Ronald's direction, but I lumbered forward, down the path. I'm a big boy for my age. Well, for any age. Out of all of us I would be the least likely to win a foot race, but the eyes were on Ronald, not me, as the gatorsauruses eased their way toward the dangling arm. Besides — the trees had called my name this time.

I got to Ronald about the same time as the closest creature saw me. Its enormous tail whipped wildly, propelling itself forward. Still in motion, I reached down and snatched Ronald's shirt by the back of his collar and pulled him with me as I went by. Ronald made a choking sound as I horse-collared him up off the pathway and back onto the rock. His arm came out of the water seconds before Sbarro pizza-slice-sized teeth chomped down it.

Ronald shuddered and coughed, making me feel better. At least he was alive. At that moment, I as much felt the light on my back as I saw that it was again getting brighter and enveloping me. The whispers, no longer entirely unintelligible, were loud, and coming at me in many different voices, both male and female. Some spoke in low, soft, soothing tones that were more like music on my ears. Others barked harsh, guttural utterances that chilled me to the bone.

"Come, young man. Come to the trees," a distinctly female voice pleaded with me.

"Get over here!" an authoritative man's voice snarled in a coarse English accent.

"What do I do?" I yelled to Mathias.

"You need to hear a secret," the old man said. "And keep it!" he added.

I nodded, turned, and made my way up to where the Grand Pines awaited me. And listened to what they had to say.

When the trees had finished with me, I made my way back down to Ronald. He was still unconscious—but breathing. Apparently satisfied, the whispers died, and the light given off by the lines of quartz quickly faded. The luminescence of the moat and vines intertwined with the wall of trees bathed the area in a scary dim greenish glow, and we realized it was dark outside the circle.

The six gatorsauruses floated evenly spaced in a line along the right side of the elevated pathway. Their eyes fixed on me—waiting. I looked them over and shook my head. "How?" I muttered softly searching my brain for a way by them. Ronald stirred—coughed, then spat a muffled curse.

A faint cracking and popping started from behind the trees. The vines had begun to retreat. The scrub oak's limbs were untwining. And the elevated path began to crumble.

Loud splashing and screaming erupted from the opposite end of the path. I looked and saw Toad, his body halfway out over the water, his ankles secure under Donnie's armpits, beating his palms on the moat's surface about twenty-feet to the right of the path. Both of them were screaming their heads off.

I started to holler for them to stop, then noticed the creatures had turned their attention to Toad and Donnie, too. And they were moving toward them. I quickly pulled Ronald to his feet and slung him over my shoulder. He grunted and I shushed him. I had to time this just right. I was slow enough by myself, but lugging Ronald also, I doubted I could outrun a sleepwalking tortoise.

The path grew narrower as the material fell away and started to reform the path that encircled the trees. I eased onto the bridge pacing myself to stay ahead of the deteriorating walkway, but behind the creatures' lines-of-sight. They had all targeted Toad as I suspected they would, and when they converged on one another, they began thrashing again.

Donnie jerked Toad out of the moat as one of the monsters propelled itself forward. He stumbled back, Toad's ankles still locked firmly under his armpits.

Toad catapulted up and over Donnie's prone body and landed with a solid thud behind him.

The gatorsauruses went wild, and I broke into a mad shamble. Ronald bounced on my shoulder, making a rhythmic guttural sound with every step. Halfway down the path, this drew the attention of the fighting monsters. They twisted and turned trying to free themselves from one another as I trudged forward on fatigued, burning legs to shouts of, "Run, Richard, run," from Donnie and Toad.

One of the creatures used the rest as an escape route and scrambled over top of them. It sprang from the mass of giant beasts and shot at the crumbling path like a torpedo. I was ten-feet away when I saw that a gap had formed between the end of the path and where we needed to be. I continued my momentum forward, reached under Ronald, and as I approached the break in the path, launched him like a shot put. He flew over the gap, slammed to the ground, and rolled to a stop.

I saw the gatorsaurus ram its nose into the space between the path and where the guys stood. The creature's jaws began to spread—then abruptly slammed shut. My foot landed on its huge nose, and I used the beast's head to cross over the missing section. I collapsed and fell to the ground when my legs gave out as I hit safety. When I looked back at the creature, I saw puny old Mathias holding the giant alligator's jaws closed. The creature backed away and disappeared into the depths of the moat.

Mathias looked at us, brushed his hands together and said, "Time to go, boys."

We walked back out the way we came, Donnie and Toad hauling Ronald between them.

It was a dreary day. The cold rain started early that morning, light at first, then heavier as the day wore on. The funeral home had been prepared. Tents were set up on three sides, and over the burial site. The rows of chairs, four deep, under the tents, were completely filled with family and friends. I watched solemnly as the six pallbearers slowly guided the casket from the hearse, to the site where Ronald's mother was to be laid to rest. He was at the front right. His brother, father, two uncles and a friend carried most of the weight.

His face was almost devoid of emotion. If anything there was anger there, not sadness. His eyes were red. He had cried, been crying—a lot since his mother passed. Through the cascading rain running down his face it was hard to tell if there were tears now.

She had gotten ill soon after that day in Two-Mile Swamp. That day the trees had told Ronald a secret. And when he spoke the name given him in confidence by whomever, or whatever spoke through, or for the trees, they had punished him. Struck him down where he stood on that rock—between those two gigantic pines.

When I went out to get him, it was my turn. But the trees didn't give me a secret—they gave me a choice. Mathias was basically telling the truth when he said the trees wouldn't hurt anyone. It was the knowledge that hurt. I saw what happened to Ronald when he shared a name. I could never tell anyone, especially not him, that when the trees gave me the choice—I chose Ronald.

TIMMY'S TALE

"ON FEBRUARY 9TH, 1973, forty-three years ago today, South Carolina was blanketed by a surprise late winter blizzard that, over a twenty-four hour period, dumped two-feet of snow across the Midlands and threw our state into turmoil for weeks.

"Forgotten in all that happened during the blizzard of 73' was the disappearance of ten-year-old Timmy Hall. Timmy had left home that day to play with friends and was never seen again. Despite the best efforts of the police, firemen, rescue workers, and volunteers who combed the Two-Mile Swamp area of Lexington County for days and weeks, no trace of little Timmy Hall was ever discovered.

"In the weeks following Timmy's disappearance, his family, friends, and a multitude of supporters held candlelight vigils, praying for the young boy's safe return. As the weeks turned to months, and months to years, the vigils became annual events that produced smaller turnouts as decades passed. Family members passed away, and the prayers offered were less for Timmy's safe return and more for information about the young boy's fate.

"Timmy Hall's younger brother, Matthew, who was five at the time of his brother's disappearance, died in 1991 during the first Gulf War. Grandparents, aunts, and uncles have all passed away over the past forty-three years. Timmy's father died tragically in a motor vehicle accident in 2013.

"Now, on this, the forty-third anniversary of his mysterious disappearance, Timmy's mother is his last living relative. Stricken with inoperable cancer and confined to her bed, Shirley Hall is under the care of hospice in her home. She remains vigilant about finding out what happened to her son, clinging to life to make one last desperate plea for information about her lost son. Her only wish—to leave this world knowing what happened to her little boy all those years ago."

Cera Michaels shudders as the television newsman's baritone voice fades and the camera pans in on the withered, bedridden Shirley Hall, mother of Timmy. The newscast has been background noise, drawing little of Cera's attention as she prepares lunch for her own son, Thomas. The mention of Timmy Hall has stopped her in her tracks. The story of the little boy's mysterious disappearance is one mothers in the neighborhoods surrounding Two-Mile Swamp have clung to over the years to frighten their own kids away from that awful place. Having been passed down for so long, the lost boy story is considered more of an urban legend by most. Cera is stunned to find out it's true, but more than anything, she wishes Thomas were there to hear it for himself.

"Here, boy," Thomas calls to the dirty, rust-colored pooch that timidly watches him from the thick brush at the edge of the swamp. "Mama says I can't go in there, boy. You'll have to come to me if you want to play."

The dog eyes him warily, alternating between wagging his stunted nub of a tail and barking playfully in short bursts. Thomas has always loved animals, especially dogs, and has wanted one for a long time, but his mother says they cannot afford a pet.

Since his father left, times have been difficult for the boy and his mother. Cera, a nurse, works extra shifts at the hospital just to keep food on the table for them, and there is little money to spare—especially for a dog.

"Please come here, boy," Thomas pleads with the dog, but the pooch stays at the edge of the woods, alternating between wagging his nub, barking, spinning around, and any other number of playful motions that beckon to Thomas.

Thomas knows, though, his mother would not want him to go into the swamp, especially alone. He has been told the story of a little boy who disappeared in the swamp a long time ago and was never seen again. He and his friends could never decide if they believed that story. There are many other tales he's heard from some of the older neighborhood boys — and their fathers. Some of those stories scare him more than the missing boy.

The name, Two-Mile Swamp, is a bit deceiving. The swamp, itself, is actually much larger. The Two-Mile part references where railroad tracks built in the 1800s dammed up one side to create an actual two-mile span of murky swamp that in areas is as much as thirty-feet deep. In the years following, dense woods, brush, and thick briars grew up all around the swamp, making passage into the area hazardous.

On top of that, stories persisted for many years prior to the boy's disappearance and since, about strange happenings, creatures, and ghosts in and around the swamp. While most people don't believe in such things, there is no denying the strange disappearance of that young boy. Rescue workers and volunteers searched the swamp for weeks but never found a single sign of him.

The *strangeness* of the swamp was at its height in the late 70s and early 80s when a creature, presumed to be a bear, caused some havoc in Peach Tree Acres, a neighborhood bordering the swamp. But as quickly as the creature appeared, it was gone, and no sign of it ever found either.

"Thom-mas," Cera Michaels calls from the house, drawing his name out into two long syllables.

He can hear his mama's voice faintly in the distance calling him for lunch. The dog's ears perk up at the sound, and he wags his little stub of a tail even more vigorously.

"That's my mama, boy. I've got to go home, but I'll be back and will bring you a treat with me," Thomas says with a huge, toothy grin.

At that, the dog's ears perk up once more, and he cocks his head to the side, as if he understands the word "treat," then wags his nub and pants just a little with excitement.

Thomas turns his head, yells, "Coming," and then runs in the direction of his house. When he looks back over his shoulder one more time, the rust-colored dog is gone.

Thomas races up to the rickety, wooden back porch steps, leaps the entire four-step distance from the bottom to the top, and lands with a thud on the deck and into the smell of his mama's grilled-cheese sandwiches wafting out through the screened back door.

His mama's grilled-cheese is the best. First, she takes a hot skillet, melts gobs of butter, then lightly grills the inside of two thick slabs of Texas Toast. She flips those over, lays in three slices of different-flavored cheeses, then sprinkles the top with a little grated Parmesan. She flips the sandwich over and over, being careful to keep the bread from getting too toasty, until the cheeses are melted into a single slab that oozes slightly over the crust of the toast. She slices that into two triangular halves and pours him a big glass of ice cold milk to wash them down.

Thomas is hungry, and Mama's grilled cheese will totally hit the spot. Most of all, he is excited and wants to get back to find the dog, back to Rusty. *Yes, that's what I will call him,* Thomas thinks to himself. *Rusty.*

"Where have you been all morning?" Cera asks as Thomas slides into his seat and grabs a triangle of grilled-cheese before his butt is even planted in the chair.

"Just playing," he says, the response muffled by a mouthful of ooey gooey goodness.

"By yourself?" she asks.

"Yep, no friends," he adds, maybe a bit too eagerly, but not wanting to give too much away. And not flat out lie to his mama. She will not like him playing with a strange dog or being so close to the swamp either. His mama is not too fond of dogs, having herself been frightened as a kid when she was chased by a pack of strays.

Like most his friend's mothers, Cera Michaels is over-protective of *her baby boy*, especially since his father left. Thomas Kinkade Michaels, Senior, was a stern man, a strict disciplinarian, but he believed in letting boys be boys, whereas Cera is very wary of the roughhousing, dirt bike-riding, football-playing boy stuff. They clashed on the subject from nearly the day Thomas took his first steps. Eventually it had torn them apart.

Thomas thinks he understands where his mama is coming from, and they have an agreement of sorts. He won't do anything that she might consider too dangerous—and what she doesn't know won't hurt her. Although that last part was his contribution, not hers.

Thomas eats so fast he practically inhales his grilled cheese but still manages to wrap the remaining triangle of his sandwich in a napkin and shove it into his coat pocket for Rusty when his mama isn't looking.

"What's your hurry?" Cera asks. "You're certainly in a big rush to get back out there."

"No hurry," Thomas says, trying to be convincing, "just having fun."

"By yourself?" Cera questions, eying him suspiciously, hands on her hips, and a look in her eye that gives Thomas pause. "Are you sure there's not something you want to tell me?"

Thomas freezes, not sure what to say. Does she know about Rusty? Has she just caught him in a lie? *Maybe I should fess up,* he thinks to himself.

"Do you have a girlfriend?" his mother asks, a wry smile spreading across her face after a brief pause that has forced a lump into Thomas' throat.

Thomas' face flushes. He is readying himself to blurt out a confession about the dog and then realizes what his mother has asked, and his cheeks go beet-red with embarrassment at the thought.

"Eew!" A red-faced Thomas spits the word out, and his face scrunches up like he has just taken a huge bite out of a lemon. "Mama, why would you ask me something like that?"

Cera chuckles, leans over to look him in the eyes, and says with a smile, "Just to embarrass you."

"Well, it worked!" he says picking up the glass of milk and draining the last little bit as he jumps out of his seat and heads toward the back door.

"Hold on, mister," Cera says opening the refrigerator, pulling out a cold bottled water, and tossing it to him. "You'll need this to wash down the rest of that grilled cheese you shoved in your pocket."

Thomas' face reddens again as he turns and catches the bottle. He had thought he slipped that one past his mom—but he hadn't. Thomas smiles sheepishly and rushes over to give his mama a big hug. "Thanks!" he says and bolts out the door.

"Be home before dark," she calls after him as Thomas flings his arm up and waves his hand to acknowledge her.

"That boy," Cera says, shaking her head, "what am I going to do with him?"

Thomas paces the edge of the swamp looking for the dirty, little pooch, but Rusty is nowhere to be found. It seems like hours pass as he whistles and calls out for the dog. He waves the triangle of the grilled cheese in the air, hoping the aroma will attract the dog's attention, but gets no response.

"Rusty," Thomas calls one last time, dragging the sound out as long as he can, his voice cracking with a mix of emotion and exhaustion. "Where'd you go, boy?" he pleads softly, and then drops his chin to his chest, tears welling up in his eyes. Defeated, Thomas turns and starts to walk away when a shuffling in the brush followed by a whimpering sound catches his attention. Thomas turns to see Rusty limp out of the swamp on three legs. His front right leg is lifted and appears injured.

"What happened, boy?" Thomas asks the dog. "How'd you hurt yourself?"

Rusty sits and licks at his leg and paw, flinching and whimpering with every touch.

Thomas moves toward him, but the dog is startled by his advance and timidly backs away into the brush.

"Aw, boy, I won't hurt you. I promise," Thomas says sheepishly, but the dog still shies away. "You don't have to be afraid of me," the boy continues. "I just want to help." But each time he tries to approach the dog, it recedes farther into the swamp. *Maybe he's afraid of boys,* Thomas thinks to himself having heard his mama talk about animals that have been abused shying away from men.

The dog again licks his leg and paw, this time whimpering louder.

"I'll get help, boy. I'll get Mama. She's a nurse. She'll know what to do. Just stay here and I'll be right back," Thomas says as the dog slowly lies down. Thomas turns and bolts toward the house.

Cera collapses into a large, cushiony chair in the living room and lets out an exhausted exhalation. She has just finished the dishes. The house is clean, and the last load of laundry is in the dryer. She glances at her phone and notices the time. *Thomas should be home any minute,* she thinks. It will be time to start dinner soon, but there is time enough for a round or twelve of Candy Crush.

With the TV on for background noise, she goes to work, again, on level 345. She has been stuck at that level for weeks. It is confounding her, with bombs, chocolate, limited moves, and an impossible order to fill. *Why did I ever start this game?* Cera sighs.

The ear-jarring sound of a Weather Alert signal blasts from the television and draws her attention away from the game just before a bomb ends the round. It has been in the mid-sixties and sunny earlier today, so the sudden weather alert is a surprise.

BREAKING NEWS: POSSIBLE BLIZZARD CONDITIONS EXPECTED WITH TEMPS IN THE SINGLE-DIGIT RANGE PROBABLE. STAY INDOORS AND BRING IN ALL PETS THAT ARE EXPOSED TO WEATHER.

"What the hell?" Cera blurts out loud, suddenly noticing a blistering cold breeze coming in through the back screen door. She jumps up from the seat, rushes to the door, and sees a quickly graying sky full of low, heavy clouds. *This makes no sense,* Cera thinks glaring at the sky. *I'm a weather junkie. I follow the forecasts. It's impossible for something like this to form out of the blue.*

With her attention so focused on the weather calamity forming above, Cera has not noticed her son barreling toward the back porch—not until the crunching sound of footfalls on packed snow falls upon her ears. Cera lowers her eyes toward the sound as Thomas bounds to the top of the steps and slides wildly on a thin sheet of ice that has formed under the snow-covered deck. She spreads her arms to catch Thomas at the same instant his feet slide out from under him and he crashes into his mother, knocking off her feet face-first into now almost a foot of soft, new snow.

"Thomas, are you alright?" Cera spits through a mouth full of snow as she pushes herself up from the deck.

"I'm sorry, Mama!" Thomas blurts. "I didn't see you!"

Cera sees tears welling in her son's eyes and turning to trickles of ice as they cascade over his red cheeks. "Get inside, Thomas. This weather is crazy and I . . . "

Thomas cuts her off, "Rusty's hurt, Mama. He's afraid of me because I'm a boy. He'll trust you. You need to help him. He'll freeze to death if you don't help him, Mama!" Thomas' angst about the dog has intensified with storm. He hurries to his feet trying to drag his mother up from the deck.

"I don't understand, Thomas. Who is Rusty? Maybe we should call his parents?" Cera asks, confused.

"No!" Thomas blurts as he tugs at his mother's hand trying to get her to follow him. "Rusty's a dog. I've been playing with him all day. He wouldn't come to me and now he's hurt. He must be afraid of boys. But you can help him. You're a girl."

Cera gets her feet under her and stands. She glances past Thomas at the whiteout conditions occurring all around them. As far as Cera can see through the sheets of falling snow in every direction, a thick, white blanket has consumed the landscape. Her eyes fall back to Thomas' stricken expression. Frozen tears and icy runnels of snot line his agonized face.

She lowers herself to one knee to look into her son's eyes, "Thomas," she starts, teary-eyed, her own features contorted with the emotional pain she feels for the child. "We can't help Rusty, not in this." Cera extends her arms out to emphasize their surroundings. "I'm sorry," she says, and leans in to hug him.

"I hate you!" Thomas screams, recoils sharply, then turns his back to his mother.

In that instant Cera feels her son's intense pain. She lowers her head to brush the tears from her own eyes and the icy trails they've formed on her frost-bitten cheeks. "Honey," Cera starts, looking up. "Thomas?" she blurts, frantically scanning the deck. But the boy is gone.

Cera darts into the house and grabs the only coat hanging on the rack by the back door—a thinly lined, nylon jacket more suited for a cool rain than the blizzard raging outside. She throws it on and rushes after her son.

Still reeling from the abrupt change in the weather and equally by Thomas' sudden attachment to this dog, Cera quickly descends the porch steps and finds two lines of long, disturbed patches of snow indicating her son's path toward the swamp. She has to hurry. The rapidly falling snow is already dusting over the trail.

Cera shivers uncontrollably as the temperature drop is undeniable. Wind gusts and frigid temperatures numb the exposed skin on her face and hands. The falling wall of snow is like wading through a waterfall. Each snowflake burns her frost-bitten flesh as the cold, wet, sticky crystals strike her face and hands. *This is crazy*, Cera thinks. *What the hell is happening?*

Her long strides through the well-worn path Thomas is making helps her move more quickly but she still cannot see him. Cera screams Thomas' name but she can barely hear herself over the gale-force winds rising up, attempting to drive her back.

Only a few dozen steps ahead of his mother, Thomas presses deeper into Two-Mile Swamp through thick briars that tug mercilessly at his clothes trying to bar his way.

Cera catches sight of her son little more than an arm's-length away. "Thomas, honey, wait for me," Cera calls out to him trying to get him to slow down, but the boy keeps trudging forward. The dense wall of falling snow continues to bury the landscape, disguising the murky outer edges of the swamp and making the path forward even more treacherous.

Cera's next few steps drive through calf-deep snow, crunch a thin layer of ice beneath, then plunge into ankle-high cold muck. The cool, muddy waters immediately soak into Cera's tennis shoes, burning and numbing her feet. She tumbles forward splaying her hands out to break her fall.

Thomas catches his mother just before she's engulfed by the soupy greenish-black melding of snow and swamp.

"Thomas!" Cera says with equal parts relief and exasperation in her voice.

"Shh, Mama," the boy says, gently covering her mouth with his bare cold hand. "Listen."

The faint sounds of barking and a young boy's voice are barely audible over the now howling winds.

"Do you hear them?" Thomas asks her. Cera nods, listening intently.

As quickly as it began, the storm rapidly subsides. The sheeting snow slows to a trickle, and Thomas and Cera's attention is drawn to the looming railroad berm before them and the playful sounds of a boy and his dog atop the massive earthen structure.

The little boy, wearing a puffy bright red winter coat, approaches the edge of the steep embankment. The dog barks frantically the closer the child gets to the edge. Cera and Thomas, at the exact same moment, see the sloughing rubble below where the boy is standing. They try to scream, but it is too late. Cera gasps and clutches Thomas to her side as the rocky edge where the boy stands evaporates. The two watch in horror as the boy slips through the void and tumbles down the embankment with the dog leaping after the child, trying to stop him from falling.

The boy cries out but is quickly silenced following a sickening thud when his head strikes a large chunk of rock protruding from the berm. The dog's pained barks resound through the swamp as the animal, half-tumbling, half-scrambling to catch the child, catches the puffy red coat in its jaws just before the point of impact and the bottom of the berm.

The dog digs its paws in, trying to slow the boy's fall, but is struck by an avalanche of rocky debris loosened by the tumble. A swath of the red material is ripped away from the boy's coat as the animal is bowled over by the rush of cascading material and thrown free from the boy, landing about twenty feet away.

Cera and Thomas wade into the thick swamp waters, trying to get close enough to help the two. They watch the injured rust-colored pooch drag itself toward the child.

Thomas sees the dog clearly now and recognizes him. "That's Rusty, Mama," he says pointing. "We're coming, boy!"

Rusty hobbles over to the boy and nuzzles his neck, but the boy lies motionless. The pooch gently licks the child's face and paws at his outstretched arm — still no response. The injured rust-colored dog lies down beside the child and curls his body around the boy, shifting and shuffling slightly to snuggle in as close to the boy as possible. Then Rusty ever so gently rests his head across the boy's head, sighs, and shuts his eyes.

Thomas pushes forward through the stinging cold muck. His mother trails close behind him. Both are unaware that their surroundings are again in turmoil. As soon as they are close enough to see the boy and the dog clearly, it's as if forty-three years pass in the blink of an eye. In a blur of motion, not unlike a vivid television sequence playing out in ultra fast forward, the boy and the dog freeze. A large section of berm sloughs down and buries their bodies. A raging blizzard covers the rocky grave, hiding it, as searchers pass in and around the area in a blurred ghostly fast forward fashion.

Weeks, months, and years, each more rapidly than the latter, pass by until another shifting of material reveals an aged puffy red coat half-buried at the base of the steep embankment.

Time slows and the frigid weather returns to the unseasonably warm February day it was before this began. Mother and son, soaked to the core, embrace.

Thomas buries his face into Cera's coat and begins to sob uncontrollably. "I'm sorry, Mama. I'm sorry I said I hate you. I love you, Mama. I love you"

Cera digs into her pocket, retrieves her cell phone, and dials 911.

"911, what's your emergency?" the robotic voice of the male operator on the other end asks.

"This is Cera Michaels. My son and I are in Two-Mile Swamp." Cera hesitates as she tries to suppress the emotion out of what she's about to say. "I think we've just discovered the remains of Timmy Hall."

WHAT IN THESE WOODS DOES CREEP?

THE LITTLE OLD CABIN in the woods had not been Nathan Roth's idea. It had been his wife, Bethany Anne, who wanted it so desperately. Built sometime in the late 1800s, the small rustic log home had character. Even Nathan had to admit that. The walls were constructed from hand-hewn logs harvested from the surrounding forest and sealed with river mud from the nearby Chattooga.

Heavy roof timbers carved out of white oak still showed the knobby protrusions from the rough-cut logs adding to the Arcadian décor. Tongue-and-groove roof decking was expertly fitted over exposed rafters and sealed with a layer of pine tar over the top, some of which had seeped into exposed joints in the roof leaving tiny dried rivulets of brownish-gold tar.

The hand-cut wooden shakes topping off the roof had been preserved well enough to survive more than a century.

The only flaw Nathan had seen in the cabin was a large circular reddish-brown stain set in the hardwood floor at the foot of the loft staircase. Bethany Anne had not seen it the same as he. She saw only beauty in the stain, saying it reminded her of a flower the way the lines fingered out from the center like petals. Nathan had thought it looked more like dried blood. Very old dried blood. And when he had questioned the grim little man who had sold them the cabin about it, he feigned any knowledge of its origin. But Nathan had never believed that.

Sadly though, after succumbing to a brief mystery illness only weeks before Nathan took possession of the deed, Bethany Anne had not survived to see it purchased. She had seen this as a summer home for the two of them. A getaway spot, and would not have approved of Nathan moving in permanently.

The truth was, Bethany Anne Roth had approved of very little her husband had done throughout their life together, and because of that, Nathan had all but abandoned his dreams long ago. Now, at the relatively young age of fifty, he found himself a widower and the beneficiary of a sizable life insurance policy.

With no children to care for, because Bethany had not wanted children, and no relatives to consider, it was an easy task for Nathan to quit his job, pull up stakes, and sell everything to move to the little cabin in the woods. Bethany would have believed this to be reckless behavior, Nathan thought to himself. He could almost hear the words in his head as if they were parting her very lips. Perhaps that was his reason for getting away. Perhaps it was precisely because Bethany Anne would not have approved.

Mostly though, Nathan wanted solitude. He wanted to be alone, away from prying eyes. He wanted to reflect on his life, his love, or lack thereof, and on his mistakes. He wanted to resurrect long-dead dreams. Breathe life back into them. He wanted to draw, he wanted to paint, and most of all, he wanted to write.

For as long as Nathan could remember, a published author was all he had aspired to be. From his earliest days growing up in Walhalla, he would weave complex, intriguing tales and recite them to his friends in such vivid detail that they would hang on his every word. Throughout his childhood, and on into adulthood, Nathan filled notebook after notebook with his ideas for stories and characters — stories and characters that would remain entombed on yellowing notebook pages after he met Bethany Anne.

Inspired by the memory of those old notebooks, Nathan rushes up the steep, narrow flight of stairs that hugs the east wall of his little cabin to the sleeping loft above. There, on a shelf in the open closet, rest the last few sealed cardboard boxes that remain unpacked. Scanning the sides of the boxes, he spots the one marked, "Nathan's stuff".

Nathan's stuff! he thinks to himself, so callously scrawled on the box's side by his wife, Bethany Anne. "This box contains so much more than just stuff," he murmurs aloud. It holds his memories, memories of a simpler, happier time in his life. It holds the focal point of ambitions and dreams that once gave him purpose. And in some way, it holds his last remaining vestige of manhood surrendered so long ago. Bethany Anne had never appreciated his ambition to do something—something creative with his life.

He grabs the box off the shelf and places it on the small wooden table in the center of the loft overlooking the living area below. Its ragged dimpled corners, scarred sides, and layer upon layer of yellowing cellophane tape do nothing to disguise its age. Nathan reflects on the last time he slit the box's bindings to reveal its contents. For a very long time, every few years or so, he would carefully cut the box open to look through its contents, drink in the memories sparked by each written page, each drawing, and each notebook it contained. The last time he had done so, he was sitting cross-legged in the crawl space under their home looking through the box when Bethany Anne came to investigate what he was doing. She scoffed at him for hanging on to such whimsical childish passions, exclaiming she had once looked at his work, and in her words, "It wasn't that good anyway."

Nathan seethed with indignation toward his wife for the biting, contemptuous tone that echoed in her words. He had always shown nothing but support for her in whatever she had endeavored to do, while never being afforded a modicum of respect for his own pursuits. Having endured so many years as the object of Bethany Anne's ridicule, Nathan may have even forgiven this transgression against his dignity, as he had so many times before, if not for what happened next.

The following morning, Nathan awoke to find that Bethany Anne had prepared a full breakfast for him. Something, as far as he could recall, she had never done before. He did not think much about it, other than she might be feeling guilty for her comment the previous day. If so, that too, would have been a first.

Breakfast was nice, but it had lasted much longer than the usual Pop Tart Nathan was accustomed to, so he was running late. The sound of air brakes outside alerted him to the arrival of the garbage truck on their street, reminding him he needed to roll the trash container to the curb. Normally, he would do this early in the morning, before heading off to work, but the breakfast had curtailed that plan as well.

"Don't worry, dear," Bethany Anne had said, her back to him, as she stood at the dining room window watching the garbage men, "I've already wheeled the container to the curb."

There was something unsettling in the manner in which she had spoken to him. It was pleasant, courteous, and respectful, all very foreign ways of communicating with him for Bethany Anne Roth. Nathan felt a flush of dread well up deep from within the pit of his stomach as he pushed back from the table and bolted for the door. The garbage man had just emptied the container into the truck and the operator was starting the compactor. Nathan screamed at them to stop, his voice barely audible over the whine of the engaged hydraulics, and looking like a mad man as he rushed the truck, waving his arms at the men. But it worked, they stopped the compactor and stepped away as Nathan dove shoulder-deep into the trash, digging frantically, eventually finding what he suspected he would. The cardboard box marked, "Nathan's stuff."

That day had changed everything for Nathan Roth. If there had been any love for Bethany Anne left in him, surely that day had stripped him clean of it. He knew now what must be done—he must be rid of Bethany Anne.

After sitting for hours on his bed, poring over every scrap of the box's contents, Nathan eventually drifts off to sleep with his memories scattered about him. He has been sleeping remarkably well since his wife's passing, and this night, his first in the little cabin, begins very much the same way. More often now, he dreams of Bethany Anne and the happier times they enjoyed together very early in their marriage. It is a difficult thing when Nathan is awake for him to recall that they actually were once in love, and both would have sacrificed anything for one another in those early days. But when he sleeps, those memories are so vividly reflected in his dreams night after night, that Nathan often awakens quite sad at the thought of his lost love, her indifferences toward him all but forgotten.

"Wake up, my love, you're in danger," Bethany Anne's voice softly whispers in Nathan's ear, jarring him from his slumber. His eyes rip wide open as he quickly springs up from the bed to a seated position, having felt his dead wife's breath upon his ear, at the exact moment he heard her warning in his dream. Shaken, Nathan paws the bed, frantically trying to find his phone to check the time. He recalls placing it on the windowsill beside his bed and brushes back the curtain to look at the digital readout, 2:44 a.m.

Outside his window, Nathan's attention is drawn to the cloudless night sky illuminated by a waning crescent moon peering over the thick pine forest that surrounds the cabin. Its pale light splashes across Nathan's property, casting contorted shadowy images along the narrow gravel drive leading to his home.

Nathan's gaze falls upon a single shadow near the corner of his outbuilding, a shadow appearing much darker than the rest and in the shape of a man standing with erect posture. Nathan presses closer to the window, focusing intently on its dark mass form, considering its eerie similarity to a human. Then, the shadow's appearance changes abruptly, and as if alerted to a presence, the solid black mass quickly squats to the ground. Shadowy arm-like limbs spring from its side, and two crouched legs take shape beneath. Its head seems to shift from side to side, then, all at once, cocks up at the window and eyes Nathan.

Overcome with fear, Nathan retreats from the window, phone in hand, and scrambles across the bed on all fours, dumping himself on the floor at the opposite side of the bed. His mind racing, he springs to his feet and darts down the stairs to make certain all the windows and doors are locked. Nathan hurries to check each lock, then huddles in the corner of the cabin farthest away from the door and dials 911.

It is nearly 4:30 a.m. when he spots the flickering blue lights preceded by a pair of headlights crawling up the long drive from the main road. There is something to be said for living this deep in the Sumter National Forest of Oconee County — then there are times like this. Between the winding mountain roads and the two-mile dirt and gravel easement that is Nathan's drive, it would take a miracle for the police to arrive in time to save him if whoever, or whatever, he saw tried to get in the cabin.

Nathan waits anxiously until the responding unit comes to a stop outside. He steps cautiously through the cabin door, walks across the porch, and descends the half-dozen steps to the driveway below. He sees one of the two officers, an older grizzled-looking man whom Nathan assumes to be the sheriff, has already exited the patrol car and is rounding the rear of the vehicle. Nathan approaches from the front to greet the other officer on the driver's side.

"Mr. Roth?" asks the deputy, who looks Nathan in the eye and puts on his uniform cap as he exits the patrol car.

"Yes, sir," Nathan responds, "thank you for coming."

"Not a problem, sir. I do apologize it took so long. But, as I am sure you are aware, it is no easy task to get out here," he says with a stern expression bordering on genuine concern. "I'm Deputy Donovan," he continues, extending a hand to Nathan. "How can I be of service to you?"

"Well," starts Nathan, shaking the deputy's hand, "I awoke at 2:44 am, looked out my bedroom window, and saw someone standing by my shed."

"What woke you?" the deputy asks, as he reaches into the patrol car, pulls out a small, black spiral-bound notebook, and begins jotting notes in it.

Nathan contemplates briefly how to answer that question. The truth, that his dead wife whispered a warning to him in his sleep, does not seem to be the appropriate response.

"It was a bad dream," he offers.

"A dream, not a noise?" asks Deputy Donovan, cutting his eyes up at Nathan from the notebook.

Again Nathan pauses, thinking maybe what he mistook for Bethany's breath on his ear was a sound from outside.

"Honestly, I can't say for certain, Deputy. I don't recall a noise, but it all happened so fast. There could have been one and I just didn't realize that's what it was."

"What can you tell me about the person you saw?" asks Donovan.

Nathan pauses again, apparently appearing dumbfounded to the deputy.

"Height, weight, clothing, skin color—anything?" Donovan asks with just a hint of annoyance creeping into his questioning.

Nathan is confounded. He saw nothing really, nothing but a shadow. And now, as he watches how clearly visible the older officer milling around the wood line behind Deputy Donovan is, even in this light, he wonders if he saw anything at all.

"It was really more of a shadow," Nathan says sheepishly, lowering his head as if the words pain him to say aloud.

Deputy Donovan looks up again from his notepad and takes a few steps toward the house.

"Is that the window you saw the shadow from?" he asks, seeding his question with a healthy dose of skepticism, as he glances up at the loft window.

"Yes," says Nathan, confident of this answer.

"Sounds like the Oconee Creeper to me," the older man chimes in from behind the deputy. Donovan cocks his head slightly, taking his eyes off the notepad to shoot a cursory glance over his left shoulder, appearing to give the older man's suggestion no more attention than he would a twig snapping behind him.

"What's the Oconee Creeper?" Nathan asks.

Donovan lets slip a barely audible sigh just before he responds to Nathan. "It's a local legend about a shadowy figure that inhabits this area. Supposedly the vengeful spirit of a lawman from these parts who was betrayed by one of his deputies for money. If you want my opinion, it was made up by moonshiners during the prohibition era to scare people out of the forest to protect their stills. Nothing you need be concerned with, Mr. Roth."

Nathan senses the deputy's skepticism has completely spiraled into outright contempt at this point, and that he does not believe Nathan saw anything.

"If you would indulge me, sir," Donovan continues, "I would like to try reenacting the situation so we can determine what, if anything, you saw tonight."

Eager to get this over with, Nathan heads back into the cabin and up the staircase to the loft. Donovan has asked Nathan to watch him through the window as he moved about the property, stepping in and out of cover, especially near the outbuilding. Nathan eases into the narrow gap between his bed and the cabin wall and sidles up to the window. He peels back the curtain, unlatches the window, pulling it up just enough for him to hear the deputy, and then nods to Donovan that he is ready.

"He's an ass!" booms a gruff voice from behind Nathan, visibly spooking him. "Oh, sorry," the voice adds, "didn't mean to startle you, young man."

"It's okay," Nathan says, quickly sizing up the old lawman and noticing his attire seems out of place — out of time even. He wears a brown leather vest with a big circular brass badge pinned to it engraved with SHERIFF inside a star at the center, dark blue jeans, a wide-brimmed cowboy hat, low-slung ammo belt and holster at his side, and a pair of boots more reminiscent of an Old West lawman than a modern-day sheriff.

Turning back to watch Donovan, Nathan says, "I didn't hear you come in."

"I'm pretty light of foot these days," the sheriff says with a chuckle. "You know he doesn't believe you," he continued in a somber tone.

"Huh?"

"Donovan, he doesn't believe you. Probably thinks you're either making this up or just plain seeing things."

Nathan listens, trying to grasp if this is some kind of tactic these two are using on him or if this man has it in for his deputy.

"He's going to tell you the shadows in these parts play tricks on your eyes. It was probably nothing and that you shouldn't worry. At worst, you might have seen a bear lurking around looking for food, and at best, it was just a shadow."

"Well, thanks," Nathan says sarcastically, "for the vote of confidence." He finishes under his breath, focusing on Donovan.

"Hey," the sheriff says, throwing up his hands, "that boy has got a lot to learn. Now me, I believe you." He sounds convincing—almost.

"Thanks," offers Nathan, although not as convincingly, now just trying to block out the old sheriff and get through this.

"No need to thank me, son," the old lawman says. "And that Creeper thing, Donovan dismisses it. But he knows as well as I do dozens of unexplained disappearances have occurred in this area."

That got Nathan's attention. "If that's true, why won't he at least acknowledge the possibility there is someone, or something out here?" he asks.

"Simple," the sheriff says, "the Creeper only feeds on bad people, Mr. Roth. You haven't done anything wrong, have you — Nathan?"

Nathan jerks, and nearly snatches the curtain off the window as he spins to look at the sheriff — but he is gone. His voice had trailed off from the gruff harsh tone that the sheriff had been exhibiting into a deep, guttural growl that culminated in a hushed whisper that was certainly Bethany Anne's voice. Nathan clenches his eyes shut, buries his palms into his eye sockets, pulls his elbows into his gut, and doubles over. He draws in a long, deep breath as he pulls himself back up, and slides his hands down his face trying to regain his composure.

Deputy Donovan, having seen Nathan rip at the curtains from his vantage point below the window and fall out of sight, unholsters his weapon and starts toward the house.

"Mr. Roth," Donovan calls as he cautiously makes his way up onto the porch, his weapon aimed forward, "are you all right in there?" He hears no response as he inches his way toward the open front door.

"Mr. Roth, can you hear me?" Donovan asks again.

"Yes," Nathan calls back as he descends the stairs and walks toward the door.

"What happened up there?" Donovan asks, holstering his pistol.

"It was something the sheriff said," Nathan tells him. "It took me off guard."

"Something the sheriff said?" Donovan asks quizzically as he eyes Nathan intently mulling over in his head what the old lawman had just said to him.

"Yes," Nathan shoots back, obviously rattled, "about the Creeper and how he only feeds on people who have done something wrong."

"Go on," says Donovan, "is there something you need to tell me, Mr. Roth?"

"Yes," stammers Nathan, "I," he pauses. "I murdered my wife, Bethany Anne, I poisoned her." And with that, Nathan Roth comes completely unhinged, collapses into a heap beside Deputy Donovan, and begins sobbing uncontrollably.

A few minutes later Nathan sits cuffed on the porch steps as Donovan checks in with dispatch to report. Over the next hour, Nathan recants his life with Bethany Anne to Deputy Donovan and a small digital recorder placed beside him. The verbal and emotional toll it took on him, and how her final contemptuous act led him to the decision to poison her.

Nathan in no way tries to portray the trauma of his marriage as justification for his actions. He knows he was wrong. His recent dreams of happier times with Bethany Anne brought to light the realization of what he had done, and Nathan is ready to atone for this.

Nathan's confession is complete, taking total responsibility, and providing Donovan with the evidence he needs to close the case—a little vial of the poison Nathan fed Bethany Anne over the preceding year. He had tucked it away in the box marked "Nathan's Stuff."

Donovan escorts his prisoner to his patrol car, sits him down in the back seat, and belts him in. The deputy takes his place behind the wheel and calls in to dispatch that he is bringing in a murder suspect. Donovan starts the vehicle and is preparing to leave the scene when he notices Nathan scanning the area outside the car with a puzzled look on his face.

"Where's the sheriff?" Nathan finally asks from behind the steel mesh separating the front and back seats.

"That's just it, Mr. Roth, I didn't bring the sheriff." Donovan says. "I came here alone tonight."

From the loft window, the ghost of Bethany Anne Roth cackles wildly as the patrolman's taillights fade away in the distance. The old lawman steps to her side.

"What are you laughing at?" he asks Bethany Anne in a deep guttural tone that chills even the spirit.

"The irony," she says, staring out the window as the morning sun begins to filter through trees.

"What irony is that?" he asks sharply.

"The irony that two spirits could ascend on a single individual to exact revenge for the same

104

horrific crime — the irony that in the end it was you, not I, that forced my husband's hand to admit his wrong doing. Though, if the choice had been mine, and mine alone, I would have seen him driven mad and forced into suicide." Bethany Anne finishes with a fiendish grin on her face.

"What is your business here anyway, spirit, in our home?" Bethany Anne asks smugly.

The lawman's human facade quickly dissolves into a thick, black liquid-like manifestation of the man. It turns to face Bethany Anne. "Your home?" Its voice booms angrily, energizing the air around her with static and rattling the timbers of the cabin.

"I built this home with my own hands," it says, the black form all at once just inches away from Bethany Anne, looming menacingly over her. "And I was murdered here. My blood, my essence still courses through these walls, giving life to this place," it continues, the dark liquid form now turbulent and swirling as the room's walls and floors tremble with each spoken word. The surroundings gradually fade into a pitch-like darkness devoid of any mass or light. Inky blue-black tendrils, crackling with energy, sprout from the emptiness that surrounds them, veining and spreading through the void like tiny vines that lash out at Bethany Anne.

"We are the Creeper!" it blurts, but the sound resonates around her as if the house itself speaks in unison with the dark spirit. "We do not seek out evil,

Bethany Anne Roth. It comes to us, and we punish it—living or dead!"

The Creeper's tendrils crawl over Bethany Anne, entangling her spirit, tugging and ripping at her form, drawing her in all directions at once as she struggles to free herself.

"*We* were not here for Nathan Roth— *we* were here for you!"

Then, with a pop, they are gone—and the cabin is empty once more.

Outside, all is quiet as the morning light presses heavily against swollen gray clouds that have gathered overhead, casting an eerie illumination on the patch of earth where the little old cabin stands. Huge droplets of rain begin to fall, slowly at first, resounding loudly as they plop against the cabin's roof until they coalesce into a heavy, drenching downpour. Rivulets of clean mountain rain form in the creases of the roof, breaking this way and that as they flow over the rough-hewn wooden shingles creating miniature waterfalls where the streams converge and cascade to the ground.

The cool rain slowly rinses away the little old cabin's pristine façade, revealing a weathered, but solid, structure aged by time and lack of care.

For a long moment, a tattered drapery at the bedroom window flutters inward as the cabin inhales deeply, drinking in the crisp mountain air. The drapery stills momentarily as a mournful sigh echoes from within the cabin, permeating through the clusters of tall pines — and the window gently slides shut.

Part Two

THROUGH THE
SWAMP

Fran Rizer

INTRODUCTION

By *Fran Rizer*

A SIX-YEAR-OLD GIRL huddled in the back seat of the two-year-old Ford sedan. She wasn't strapped in with seatbelts because cars didn't come with them back then. She wedged her red curls against the rear passenger door and closed her eyes, intending to nap on the way from Sumter, South Carolina, to her home in Columbia. The pitter-patter of rain and the slap-slap-slap of the windshield wipers provided her lullaby.

The child tuned out the conversation between her mother and father until Daddy addressed her directly. "Fancy, is your door locked?" he asked.

"Yes, sir," the girl answered as she sat up and pressed the little knob down.

"I don't like you leaning against the door with it unlocked," Mama said.

"Your mother is right. Always lock up so you won't fall out," Daddy said, "but that's not the only reason when we ride through the swamp."

Fancy wasn't quite sure what a swamp was, but if Daddy felt it necessary to keep it out of the car, it must be something worth seeing. She rolled down the window with the crank that would, years later, be replaced in newer cars by power windows the driver could control.

"Put that window up, Fancy," Daddy snapped. His tone was not one the little girl was accustomed to hearing from her father.

"I was looking at the swamp," the youngster protested. "It's scary-looking with all those trees and shadows. Is that water on the ground?"

"Yes, but the trees aren't going to hurt you. I just don't want to pick up the ghost."

"Now, don't go telling her stories and scaring her. She's just a child," Mama said.

"She's old enough to know."

So far as Fancy knew, ghosts were kids wearing white pillow cases over their heads on Halloween, but Daddy continued. "Years ago, a newly-wed husband and wife were traveling this road from Sumter to Columbia."

"Were they going on their honeymoon?" Fancy asked.

"No, they were coming back from eloping to get married in Sumter. She didn't have a wedding gown, but she'd married him in a new white dress. The man was in construction like me, and he was taking his bride back to her mama and daddy's before he left to go to work in Georgia for the week."

"Aren't you working in Georgia next week?" Mama asked.

"Yep, down in Jesup."

"So they were going home to Columbia like us?" Fancy questioned.

"Yes, on this very road, and it was raining—just like it is now."

"What happened?"

"The next year on that same day . . ." Daddy grinned at Mama before continuing, "a man was traveling on this road when he saw a hitchhiker—a young woman wearing a white dress. When he stopped and she got into the car, she asked, "How far are you traveling? I need to go all the way to Columbia." He paused. "The girl in white told them an address downtown on Pickens Street."

"Please," Mama interrupted, "you're going to scare her, and she won't be able to sleep tonight."

"She's old enough to understand this." He turned toward the back seat. "Aren't you, Fancy?"

Definitely a Daddy's girl, Fancy said, "Yes, and I promise to go to bed without crying."

Daddy returned to the story. "The hitchhiker sat silently in the back seat all the way to Columbia. When they parked in front of the address she'd named on Pickens Street and the man turned around, the back seat was empty."

"Did she sneak out?" Fancy asked.

"No, the car had been moving all the time since the man picked her up. He walked up on the porch and knocked on the door. An elderly lady opened it. After the driver told her what happened, she said, "My daughter died in an auto accident on the edge of the swamp on the Sumter Highway one year ago today. I guess she's still trying to come home.""

Daddy raised his eyebrows and gave Mama and Fancy a wicked grin. "Since then, on the anniversary of that long-ago accident, someone driving across the swamp bridge picks up a hitchhiking woman who disappears from the car before they reach her home on Pickens Street." He looked out the window and pointed.

"Oh, look," Daddy said, "there's the house.""

The little girl shivered with fear and ducked down

to avoid looking where her father pointed.

I was that red-haired child, and I believed every word my father said when I was that age. Since then, I've learned the story is not unique to Columbia, South Carolina. With other towns, other roads, and other addresses, stories of vanishing hitchhikers have been told not only since the twenty-first century, but also during horse and buggy days in America and Europe.

Check out YouTube Music for several recordings, including an excellent one by Charlie Waller and the Country Gentlemen, performing, "Bringing Mary Home." It's the same vanishing hitchhiker story told in a song written by Joe Kingston, Chaw Monk, and John Duffey in 1969.

In Part One of the first edition of *Southern Swamps and Ruins*, Richard D. Laudenslager took readers on a journey through Two-Mile Swamp. My introduction for Part Two is a true memory of my father first instilling a love for swamps and ghost stories in me while riding through the swamp when I was six years old, but this section is not a memoir, and not all of my tales take place in swamps. Two of the stories are adaptations of real events that happened in my family. Come with me to visit my kin, my friends, and the strange beings that go bump in the night in South Carolina.

EMILY'S GHOST STORY

This story previously appeared in the Spring, 2013, issue of Pages of Stories, *Canada.*

I SIT SILENTLY as Drew drives our red Porsche along the rutted dirt road. It's been three days since he spoke to me this time. Seventy-two hours of quiet. An eternity of longing to hear him say my name — "Emily." I hated that word until I met Drew. The people in South Carolina's low country drop the "i," and it comes out Emm-lee.

The first time I ever saw Drew, I'd gone to put flowers on Grandma's grave for her birthday. That always made me sad because I still missed her, so I then stopped by the burned-out ruins of the Old Sheldon Church in Yemassee. I was upset. Going to St. Mary Cemetery where Grandma and Daddy were buried always made me cry. For some reason, walking around the beautiful Sheldon Church Yard with the huge oaks draped in Spanish moss sometimes made me stop weeping and feel peaceful. People were buried there, too, but most of those graves were from the 1700s and 1800s — not people I had known and loved.

Drew was in the churchyard sketching moss-covered trees and the remains of the structure. I stood behind him and watched as he created a whole world out of just a few pencil strokes. After several moments, he turned and looked at me with unwavering blue eyes. The man took my breath.

"Who are you?" he asked. Sometimes I'm flippant, downright sarcastic. Got an attitude. It's a wonder I didn't answer, "What's it to *you*?"

Instead I replied, "I'm Emily."

"Emily as in Emily Dickinson?" he asked, and I laughed with pure pleasure. He'd pronounced my name with three delicate syllables. It sounded positively delicious when Drew said it.

"Yes," I answered, "but I don't make up poetry. I try to write stories."

"Why *try*? Why don't you just write them?"

"I don't know. I guess I'm not too good at it yet."

"You can be if you want to be," Drew said, and his words encouraged me, making me feel happy with myself.

* * *

That's how it began. Before long, we were spending most of our time together. Lots of days sitting side by side in churchyards or marshes. Me writing my little tales on a yellow legal pad while Drew sketched or painted.

"What are you writing?" Drew asked.

"A story to send to a magazine. I need to see my words in print. I want people to read what I write."

"Where did you get the idea?"

"I made it up. It's about a boy and girl falling in love and seeing a ghost."

"Oh," Drew said and went back to drawing.

When it rained hard and we couldn't sit outside, we escaped into Drew's battered old van. He kept a collection of Andrew Wyeth prints there. During bad weather and at night, Drew showed them to me.

"I want to paint like Wyeth!" he exclaimed. His eyes lit up like he was on fire inside. "When Wyeth paints fog and wind, you can *feel* them! Just look at this print. It's called 'Sea Fog.' You can *see* the mist beginning to drift, to wisp away. You can feel the breeze tease your shirt in 'Wind from the Sea.' That's how I'm going to paint!"

I didn't have any books of my own, just the ones I checked out from the library. I'd hold up one of my favorite collections of short stories – *Everything's Eventual* by Stephen King – or one of Edgar Allan Poe's and say, "Someday I'm going to write like this – mysteries and about ghosts and spooky things."

"But, Emily, you've never experienced any of that. Write about the life you've lived, people like the ones you know."

I tossed my head to swing my hair back. "Don't tell me what to do!" I snapped at him.

Drew turned away from me and looked at his Wyeth prints again. He loved them all, but his favorite painting was "Christina's World." Everyone's seen the picture of a young woman in a field of grass looking up toward a clapboard house and barn on top of a knoll. The girl's wearing a pink dress, and her position looks strange. It's as though she's crawling, but her body seems twisted.

"That's Christina Olson," Drew explained. "She was crippled from childhood. Wyeth painted her and that farm for almost thirty years." The picture has a haunting quality." Drew added, "It merges a feeling of loss and a sense of fulfillment at the same time." At first, I thought that was ridiculously impossible, but now it makes sense.

When Drew decided we should live together, I told him that wasn't how my Mama raised me, so we got married. Drew started selling paintings, and I mailed some of my stories off to magazines. I cried a lot the first year. Every time the mailman delivered a rejection letter, I sobbed. Mama always scolded me, "Don't carry on so!" and I'd wail even louder.

My husband comforted me. He held me in his arms and gently brushed the hair away from my eyes. He kept telling me, "Quit worrying about writing proper by some teacher's rules and making up supernatural stories about vampires and witches. Your stories about ghosts and murders sound too manufactured, too made up. Keep your stories *real*. Write those funny things you've told me about your relatives and low-country people, and put them on paper the same way you tell them." I sniffled when he added, "And you can stop studying the dictionary to learn bigger words. Convey those yarns in your own vocabulary."

I argued with him. "No magazine or book is gonna publish those stories," I whined. "I want to write about the paranormal."

Usually I go on and do things my own way when people try to tell me what to do, but I got turned down every time I sent out a manuscript. I finally decided to try Drew's suggestions. I wrote an old family anecdote of how my grandparents always killed a couple of chickens for Thanksgiving because they didn't raise turkeys and couldn't afford to buy one. Finally the year came when they bought a big bird from the store – a Tom, the biggest frozen turkey available. Grandma put it on the back porch to thaw. When she went back to check on the bird, she found their big ole cat named Tom chowin' down on that Tom turkey. Grandma used to say, "If Grandpa'd had his way, we'd of had roasted Tom cat for Thanksgiving that year." I mailed the story off to a regional magazine.

You could've heard me hollering in the next county when the mail man brought an envelope with a check inside. When I followed Drew's advice and wrote the stories like I told them, checks and contracts kept coming instead of rejections. Drew told me what to write and sometimes tried to tell me how to write. He'd brush my bangs out of my eyes and say, "Don't you think it's time you started writing on a computer instead of with a pencil?" I didn't switch to writing on the computer, but I did use the Dell he bought me to type up my stories after I wrote them on the yellow pads.

My work was even reviewed in newspapers and a couple of magazines. That was good. The bad thing was that they called me "folksy" and referred to me as a young literary Grandma Moses -- like writing and painting are comparable!

Drew refused to see why that made me mad. He said, "You should be happy and proud," but I tried to explain that all I'd done was follow his directions. I felt like it was *his* accomplishment, not *mine*. He was an artist! Where'd he get off telling me how to write?

Paintings kept selling, too. We were as excited as kids on the last day of school when he had his first show at an art gallery in Charleston. Drew said, "I can't wear paint-splattered jeans," and bought himself a new outfit with a sports jacket. He gave me money for a dress, but he didn't like anything I picked out. Finally, Drew bought a dress and brought it home. I tried it on, and Drew said it was "perfect." I couldn't see wearing black anywhere except to a funeral, but he just laughed and said, "It's a classic, your first little black dress." He gave me a necklace to wear with it. Not dime-store beads, *jewelry* store pearls!

We moved out of my mama's house and rented a place of our own. Most of that time was happy for me, and I think for Drew, too. I still liked to go with him when he went out sketching, and even then, he listened when I talked about stories I wanted to write. Sometimes I'd take along a book like *Ghosts of South Carolina* and read instead of writing. I learned about dozens of apparitions in our state, and when I told Drew about the phantom hitch hiker on the Sumter Highway or the Gray Ghost on the coast who warns of hurricanes, he listened. We even went together to Edisto Island and visited a crypt that was said to be haunted and a tree that is rumored to have a pirate specter guarding treasure buried beneath it. Drew was the most patient man I'd ever known and never complained about me babbling on or wanting to sit and wait to see if a spirit would appear.

Before long, we started making *real* money selling his pictures and my stories. I have to confess my ghost stories didn't sell, but the simple low-country ones did. That's when Drew decided he wanted to move back to Maine. I screamed, "What's wrong with painting swamps and marshes?" but he didn't answer me.

Drew told folks I won that skirmish because we moved upstate, which was a lot closer to my home place than Maine. So far as I was concerned, I'd lost anyway. It wasn't that I didn't want to move to Maine. I didn't want to move *anywhere* away from the coast of South Carolina!

The Greenville Museum of Art is home of an impressive permanent collection of Andrew Wyeth's work. When CNN told us Wyeth had died at age ninety-two, Drew insisted we make a road trip from Beaufort to see the exhibit. He stood in awe before each piece. "Why are you staring like that?" I asked. "I don't see one bit of difference between this stuff and your prints."

"These are the real thing. It's like being in the presence of a lifelong hero." Tears welled in his eyes. "I always planned to travel to meet the man someday, but I waited too long. All I can do is visit his work."

I looked at my watch. "It's past lunchtime," I said. "Let's go find a restaurant."

Drew shook his head and looked at me with disbelief, but I kept complaining about how hungry I was, so we finally left. In my opinion, it was a long ride for nothing. I had no idea that useless day trip would be a major part of deciding where we'd live. A week later, Drew disappeared for several days. When he came back, he said "we'd" bought a three-story clapboard house on a hill a little north of Greenville. I screamed and hollered, but we moved there anyway.

The studio he contracted to have built looked like a farm shed. The new garage in the back was a fake barn, and Drew scolded me when I didn't park in it. By the time I'd followed around the road that circled our hill to the one driveway that led up to the house, I wasn't in the mood to continue around our home to park in the barn.

"Always park inside and close the doors," he said. "New vans and sports cars around our home don't fit the picture!"

Drew cut down the beautiful old trees around the house and had wheat planted in the stark, bare fields. Our farmhouse was exactly like a picture postcard of "Christina's World" without Christina. Sometimes I thought Drew would be happy if I were crippled like she was. Maybe then he'd paint *me*. In all our years together, he'd never drawn or painted my likeness. He claimed he didn't do portraits, and I never saw people in his work, but it still made me mad. He always told me what to do – write this way, stand that way. I told him, "If I was good enough for you when you met me, I'm good enough for you now, because I'm not gonna change!"

His answer was usually a muttered, "Most folks grow up eventually."

Then the quiet times came. I call them quiet times, but the silence is one-sided. Drew stops talking to me, but I continue speaking to him. When I wake up in the morning and hear the birds singing outside and see the sunshine kaleidoscoping patterns on the walls through the lace curtains, I always lean over to kiss Drew and tell him about whatever I plan to write that day. Most times he listens and then kisses me, too, but when he's having a quiet time, he turns his back to me.

Drew doesn't answer when I call him for breakfast during a quiet time. He comes into the kitchen and sits down at the big, round oak table. He eats whatever I've cooked for him with no comments about whether he likes it or not. Doesn't seem to matter if it's chicken-fried steak, eggs with cheese and scratch biscuits or simply grits with bologna gravy. Never says a word to me during quiet times. Just eats, then gets up and goes to his studio or climbs in his shiny new van and drives away for the day.

I wonder if he's out sketching and painting or if he's gone to the museum to "visit" his beloved Andrew Wyeth paintings.

Watercolors of dilapidated, falling-down barns have been selling like McDonald's quarter-pounders. Drew's even painted some old crypts and graveyards around Greenville, and those pictures have been pulling in big money, too. I don't think it's fair that he tells me not to write about ghosts or graves and things like that, but he does those cemetery paintings. When I stomp my feet and tell him how I feel, he ignores me.

Lately, it seems we're having quiet times more than ever. I'd think he'd be happy that he's successful, but who can tell? He never complains about anything, so how do I know whether he's angry, disappointed, or just sad? He looks at me different, too. He narrows his eyes, and the intensity of his art is in those blue slits. Those cold, blue eyes freeze me so bad I just shiver.

Now we're riding in the Porsche with the top down. He hasn't said a word all the way back from an art show at some hifalutin gallery in Atlanta. Actually, it's been three days since Drew spoke to me. The longest quiet time was almost two weeks. I wonder how many days and nights this one will last. What caused it? Most times he doesn't seem to notice me at all anymore, but the night of the opening reception, he kept glaring at me. During the first hour, he told me to stand up straight so many times that I got mad and left. I went out and sat in the car.

Thank heaven we're almost home. I look ahead and see our lonely house sitting atop the bare hill surrounded by fields of wheat that look like dried grass. A delicate breeze whispers a warning through the wheat, but I ignore it.

"A lot of your work at that show was those cemetery pictures," I say, "but you always tell me that my mystery and ghost stories aren't as good as the stories about my family and folks living on the coast. I don't think that's fair." He stays silent. "Why don't you paint people?" I demand.

Drew doesn't say anything, just keeps driving.

"It's taking forever to get there," I say. "You should have a driveway cut from the house down to the road on this side instead of having to ride all around the hill before we get to the turnoff. I'm so tired of everything having to look like the Olson farm."

Drew keeps driving, his white-knuckled fingers clenched tight against the steering wheel. His eyes stare straight ahead, and his jaw works -- flex and release, flex and release.

"Hurry up!" I say, "I need to use the bathroom!"

Unexpectedly, Drew turns off the road before we reach our long driveway. We're hurtling across the field, headed toward the house.

"Stop!" I yell at him. "You're going too fast!"

Drew slams his foot on the accelerator. The low undercarriage of the Porsche drags against the plowed furrows of the field shearing off wheat and flinging it into the air. The car lurches to a stop. Drew stomps the accelerator even harder. Tires spin, and dust flies up all around us. Slowly, he turns in his seat and faces me. For the first time in my whole life, I know real fear. My heart thunders in my chest. A scream rises in my throat, but I choke it down, and no sound escapes me. Drew stares at my face with a fixed expression. His features are unfathomable. Insanity or evil? I can't distinguish. His eyes squint, and I recognize the emotion.

Only one word describes his look: loathing. The man I love despises me. Suddenly, I know this. I don't have to think about it. There's no doubt. The man I love hates me! I fling my car door open, get out, and run toward the house. Drew jumps from the Porsche and follows me. I stumble over a rock and gasp as the breath whooshes out of me. Just as I hit the ground in a sprawl, he grabs me.

Do you know what a space break is? It's one of those double spaces to show that time has passed in a story. I have a space break in my life. One minute I'm tumbling to the ground with Drew clutching me. The next thing I know, I'm standing on the little front porch of our house. I have no idea how I got to the steps, no memory of climbing the hill.

Drew is right in front of me. He goes in and leaves the door wide open. I'm standing on the small stoop.

I lean against the door frame for a moment before following him into the front hall. He paces around inside the house, from room to room, up the stairs, down the stairs, pausing to gaze at each framed Andrew Wyeth print on the walls. He stops and pats his favorite chair just like Grandpa used to pet his favorite hound dog.

My husband walks toward me, and I shout, "Talk to me! Stop this foolish silence! I'm tired of being ignored." The look on Drew's face chills me, and I shiver. His sad eyes seem to see right past me. There's no expression at all. Suddenly I realize that I'm screaming.

"Drew," I lower my voice almost to a whisper, "we have to do something to save our marriage." He ignores me. "I'm not putting up with any more of this!" The words leap from my mouth, growing louder and louder. Before I know it, I'm yelling again. "I *said* I can't go on this way!" When Drew reaches the door, I move directly in front of him, blocking his way. Drew steps right *through* me!

Now I know. I finally comprehend. An epiphany. Lights flash on abruptly in my mind. Drew murdered me! Killed me right out there in the field of wheat on the slope of the Christina's World we live in, though I don't guess I really *live* here anymore. I'm experiencing a real murder and ghost, but what good will that do me since I'm the ghost myself?

For the rest of Drew's life, I will haunt him. I

loved him. I loved him more than any woman ought to care about a man. That's how low-country females are. Why am I using past tense? I *still* love Drew. I love the way he used to hold me and whisper, "I died for Beauty—but was scarce adjusted in the Tomb when one who died for Truth was lain in an adjoining room." That's from Emily Dickinson. I know the words don't sound romantic, but when Drew said it very softly with his lips barely brushing against my ear, it was incredibly sweet and sexy. He hasn't done that in a long time.

Drew exits through the open front door. I shadow right on his heels, but he doesn't see me. I'm dead. I follow him as he crosses the porch and starts down the hill to the field. Is he going for the car? I don't think he's planning to bury me—he didn't get the shovel. Why did he go around gazing at everything in such a final, sorrowful way like he was saying goodbye? Will he drive away to Maine before my body is discovered?

Now we're near where it happened. I can see the wheat flattened in a spot about thirty feet from the Porsche. Drew reaches the area before I do. He stands there, solemnly looking down. What's he feeling? Is he overwhelmed with grief, or is he glad to be rid of me?

As I plod the final few feet to stand by Drew, horror greater than I've ever known floods over me. I'm scared to see my body. Terrified to stand beside the man I love as he stares at my corpse on the ground. I tremble. I'm afraid to see myself in death. Will I look like a bloody, twisted Christina? Even now, I want to be attractive for Drew, so pretty that he'll regret what he did. I want him to cry for me, miss me, *love* me! I wish he would say something, but then, he doesn't know my ghost is standing right by him. Besides, he's not talking to me these days, anyway.

I look down. The body lies motionless. The head is bloodied, and a wet, crimson-stained rock, the weapon of destruction, lies close by. This simple stone has ended all chances of saving our marriage.

The corpse is not me.

My beloved Drew lies dead at my feet. I look at my hands and see his blood. Then I scream and scream as the phantasm standing beside me drifts away like fog in a fine Andrew Wyeth painting.

ROSES FOR AMANDA

"LOOK," Misty, the school secretary, said as she entered Amanda's classroom Friday afternoon carrying a vase filled with red roses and white baby's breath. "Somebody's sweetheart must have done something awful if it's not your birthday or the anniversary of your first date!"

"They're beautiful," Amanda agreed, "but somehow the bouquet isn't as impressive when the gentleman who sent them owns a florist shop and roses are his personal favorite flower." She slipped the card from the envelope, read it, then grinned at Misty and continued, "And even less exciting when the reason for sending roses is that he's taking a rain check on our weekend plans."

"Cancelling?" Misty asked. "I thought you two were headed for the mountains tonight. I'm surprised you didn't slip out of here the minute the kids left. It's all you've talked about—a weekend in Asheville and another tour of the Biltmore Estate and their rose garden." Misty laughed self-consciously. "I swear, Amanda, you should live in North Carolina instead of South Carolina!"

"I'd love to live in Asheville, but Dwayne's business is here, and we're serious enough that I don't want to move away from him."

"I've seen the way he looks at you when he comes by the school. You're right to stay here. I think this relationship is the real thing." Misty leaned over Amanda's shoulder. "What does the card say?"

Amanda handed the small white square to Misty, who read it aloud. "So sorry, but Rollin is sick, and I'm driving for him. Please give me a rain check on Asheville 'til next weekend. Love, Dwayne. . . PS – Every time you smell the fragrance of roses, think of me."

Misty looked up at Amanda. "What does he mean when he says he's driving for Rollin?"

"That friend of his who races cars. Dwayne has subbed for him a couple of times before—nothing big, just competitions about fifty miles away."

"Why doesn't Dwayne invite you to go with him?"

"He knows how I feel about racing. It's a dangerous sport. I'd be a nervous wreck all weekend." She sniffed one of the roses. "They do smell good, don't they?"

As sad as Amanda remembered feeling that Friday afternoon, her gloom paled to nothing in comparison with what happened next. Though he'd driven for Rollin a few times before, Dwayne wasn't an experienced race driver. The car spun out, crashed into a concrete wall, and burst into flames. Even with his helmet, Dwayne suffered severe brain damage and destruction of his face. He'd lingered for several weeks before his family made the heartbreaking decision to disconnect life support. Dwayne died in only a few minutes.

Amanda would never forget the horror of that awful weekend and the sight of Dwayne hooked up to monitors and tubes, but the funeral visitation remained her worst memory. Rather than request a closed casket, Dwayne's family had allowed the top half of the coffin to be open, but since the cosmetician was unable to rebuild Dwayne's face satisfactorily, the body had been displayed with the head wrapped in gauze—like a mummy or a butterfly cocoon. The mortuary had been filled with so many funeral sprays with roses that the cloying scent overwhelmed Amanda.

Two years of grieving passed before Amanda began dating again, and then she made sure each man knew that she never wanted to receive roses for any reason whatsoever. The sweet scent of that particular flower made her weep with renewed grief.

Twenty years later, Amanda was contented though not so ecstatically happy as she might have been if Dwayne had lived to become her husband and the father of her child. As it was, Jake was a generous man who loved and spoiled both Amanda and their son Joshua.

The few arguments Amanda had with her husband were generally about Josh. Amanda's husband liked cars. He and Amanda both drove BMWs, but Jake was adamant that the perfect gift for their son's sixteenth birthday was a sporty vehicle.

"Amanda, I've found the car for Josh," Jake insisted. "Baker's Chevrolet has a new silver Corvette, and I'm getting a great deal on it."

"A Corvette!" Amanda exploded. "Josh just got his driver's license. I don't want him in a sporty car that will encourage him to speed or show off. Wasn't that old movie star James Dean killed in a silver Corvette?"

"No, Mandy, that was a Porsche and over fifty years ago. This is a Vette, and Josh is a very level-headed young man. I'm proud of him and want him to know it."

"I think he's too young for a sporty car. Get him a sensible car now and a Corvette when he graduates," Amanda argued. She had more to say and she said it, but on Josh's birthday, he found his gift parked in the driveway—a silver Vette with a gigantic red bow on the hood.

Only two weeks after his birthday, Amanda experienced every mother's nightmare.

"Be careful driving in this rain," she said to Josh as he climbed into the Vette.

"Sure, Mom," her son called and drove off.

Amanda had another cup of coffee before grabbing her book bag and umbrella. Jake was out of town on business, so she turned off the lights, locked the door, and carefully pulled out of the driveway. The rain was worse than she'd thought.

Half a mile from the house, Amanda saw blue lights flashing. Police cars, fire trucks, and ambulances surrounded the overpass. Amanda's heart pounded with fear as the single open lane of traffic inched forward around the accident. She felt like she'd die herself when she was waved around the incident and saw the silver Corvette smashed into the concrete abutment.

Amanda didn't know much about cars, but she knew there weren't many silver Corvettes in their small town — probably only one still wearing a paper temporary tag. The front of the car was shredded with the driver's side of the roof torn off.

Amanda slowed to a stop and pressed the button to lower her window. The rain pelting her through the open space felt like bullets. "That's my son's car!" she screeched frantically at the officer who tried to wave her around. She didn't have to tell him twice. He cleared the way for her to pull out of the slow-moving lane of traffic, then leaned over and told her, "Go to that police car right there." He pointed and added, "It's the damnedest thing we've ever seen."

Horrified with fear she'd be told that Josh had been smashed and was trapped in the car, Amanda parked and walked through the rain toward where the officer pointed.

She couldn't believe what she saw. Joshua sat in the front seat beside a patrolman. Amanda couldn't see a scratch on her son.

"That's my mom!" Josh cried out, opened the passenger door, and scooted over toward the officer.

Amanda slid in beside Josh and gasped, "I don't understand. You don't look hurt."

"It's the craziest thing," the patrolman said. "When I pulled up, I was sure someone was killed in that car. Your son was sitting in the passenger seat, but he swears that while he was driving, his seat belt unlocked, and he was pushed out of the driver's seat just at the moment of impact."

"That's what happened, Mom!" Josh said.

The officer looked at Amanda and then at Josh. "Are you sure we won't find a young lady in that car? It smells like a bottle of perfume broke in there."

"I was alone," Josh insisted. "I'd just left home all by myself. The car hydroplaned and I couldn't control it. I saw I was going to hit the concrete, but suddenly I was thrown to the other side, and that odor filled the car."

The Vette was a total loss, but that afternoon Amanda went with her husband and son to the junkyard to get Josh's book bag. Even with the roof torn off and the front quarter shredded, the car smelled to high heaven. The police insisted there had to have been a bottle of cologne or a rose-scented air freshener in the car to leave that odor. Amanda wondered about it until she looked in the passenger seat where her son had survived the crash. A tiny piece of cloth lay there—a scrap of white gauze.

POSITIVE PROOF

This story won a Porter Fleming Award in Fiction and was previously published in the spring, 2014, issue of Ficta Fabula, *Ontario, Canada.*

EVELYN HILLSHIRE remembered the day Kennedy died. Not Bobby. Jack. She'd admired both Kennedys, but she *adored* John. Neither five decades nor rumors could diminish her infatuation with the American Camelot of the sixties. Now all the to-do about the fiftieth anniversary of President Kennedy's assassination fascinated her and helped fill the long, lonely days of her seventieth year.

Tonight the only sound and light in Evelyn's bedroom at Pretty Pines Assisted Living came from the television. The CNN commentator's voice held her attention. "The animated gifs and most recent computer-enhanced version of the famous Zapruder film made at the Kennedy assassination still does not provide proof beyond a reasonable doubt . . . "

No real proof after fifty years, thought Evelyn as she took off her glasses, placed them on the bedside table, and reached for the remote to turn off the TV. She froze when the broadcaster continued, "Tonight we also have a film that has never before been shown to the public. Due to a quirk of fate, this footage that might have given positive proof about a second assassin on the grassy knoll does not provide that evidence. Watch carefully. The camera was focused on the knoll, but the photographer turned just at the moment of the assassination."

The film was short. First it panned the crowds, next moved slowly across the grassy knoll, focused briefly on a man standing there holding something, and then moved rapidly to zoom in on the face of a child—a blond-haired boy of nine or ten. The image jerked suddenly, went out of focus, and became clear again as it showed the open limousine with the fatally wounded President.

"As you saw," the news man continued, "this film clearly establishes a man on the knoll, but that excellent human interest shot of the youngster is all that can be seen at the actual moment of the shooting. If the camera had stayed focused on the knoll, history would be more complete concerning the fateful . . ."

Evelyn didn't hear any more. As intriguing as the Kennedy tragedy was, her attention was drawn to the boy's face, uncannily like the features of another small boy. Her mind moved back ten years to her brief time with Cephas, a tragedy in his own right.

In 2003, after Evelyn retired from full-time teaching, she'd been asked to substitute on Surcie Island off the coast of South Carolina while Mr. Kelly, the regular teacher, recovered from surgery. Surcie School, one room on an island way behind the times, was a drastic change from Evelyn's years teaching in the city. To Evelyn, divorced with grown children gone their own ways, it sounded like an adventure, and she'd accepted the September through November assignment.

The first morning went fine. Evelyn introduced herself and played a few icebreaker games. After lunch she began actually teaching. She clearly remembered the words that had brought little Cephas to her attention.

"Hey, Teacher," a child interrupted. "Cephas is having one of his fits, and you ain't got no place for him to lay down."

Not sure which one was Cephas, Evelyn scanned the room, looking for a child in the throes of a grand mal seizure, but the children were all staring at a little tow-headed boy in a faded red shirt, head on his desk. She walked to him, touched him.

"He's just asleep," Evelyn tried to assure the children.

"No, ma'am. He's havin' one of his fits. When he wakes up, he won't know where he is, and his head's gonna hurt awful. Mr. Kelly always has a pallet for Cephas to lay down on."

"Cephas is a retard," another child piped up. "He has fits, and he can't never answer no questions about what we learn."

Evelyn hadn't heard the term "retard" in years. She didn't try to explain the current term was "challenged." Instead she told the students to think of Cephas as a "special" boy and not to say "retarded." She talked to them of kindness and understanding. Then she let the children help her find the pallet in the closet and spread it out in the corner for Cephas.

The child awoke with a start. He put his hands to his head and sobbed, looked to the corner, slipped from his chair, and crawled to the pallet like a wounded animal. He lay there more than an hour, a pathetic little creature, silently weeping with his palms pressed fiercely to his temples. He left with the other children at the end of the day.

After dismissal, Evelyn looked up Cephas's emergency card, seeking information—the name of the child's doctor; what, if any, medication he was taking. Nothing that should have been on the card was there. Not a word about his epilepsy. She was certain that's what it was, some form of epilepsy.

Cell phone reception on the island was non-existent. The only telephone that worked was at the store. Evelyn called Mr. Kelly on the mainland from there, painfully aware of the lack of privacy. Kelly was no help at all. He said Cephas didn't have the spells too often. He advised Evelyn to just let the child rest after each episode. When Evelyn questioned Kelly about medical supervision, he'd informed her that she didn't understand these people. There was no medical care on the island. A trip to the nearest clinic meant a boat ride and loss of a day's wages to the residents of Surcie Island.

"Furthermore," he added, "when the district nurse came to the island and made a home visit, the boy's mother became angry, mentioned taking the boy out of school, and finally threatened to 'whup some ass,' if anybody 'messed' with Cephas." Kelly's parting advice: "You don't understand island culture. Leave it alone. I'll be back the end of November."

Evelyn tried to follow the teacher's advice, but Cephas tugged at her heartstrings. She developed a habit of letting him stay after school a few minutes to help her. He obviously liked this, but she couldn't get him to open up about himself or the seizures.

As she lay down and pulled the bedcovers up around her, Evelyn remembered one of her favorite times at Surcie Island — the afternoon Cephas brought live crabs to her house. They cooked and ate together that evening. It was one of the few times Cephas really talked to her.

Cephas remembered that day, too. Teacher Lady had commented that morning that she'd never eaten the crabs so common to the islanders. He mentally checked off the times involved. The tides. Then he closed his eyes, knowing the effort would cost him. He'd escaped into one of his fits the day before. The after-storm was always worse if he did it frequently, but Teacher Lady had never eaten crabs, and she was kind to him.

"Minus means the same as take away," the teacher's voice droned.

Eyes clenched tightly, Cephas put his head on his desk. *Simpson Creek. Simpson Creek,* Cephas thought. *Today. Now. Simpson Creek.*

In the hollowed tree, Cephas found rope, his crab box, and thick string with aged chicken necks still tied to the end. He rolled up his pants legs and waded into the cool tidal creek water. Slowly and carefully, Cephas walked to the end of the string, lifted it, and dumped the scrabbling crabs into his box. Soon the crab box was full.

Cephas used one end of the rope to tie the lid tight on the box. He lowered the box into the water and tied the other end of the rope to a tree branch. He stored the string and smelly chicken necks in the tree hollow, rolled down his pants legs, then closed his eyes tightly.

Classroom. Today. Now. Classroom.

Evelyn had been aware of Cephas's attitude of

sleep. She was now teaching reading but repeatedly looked toward his desk, waiting for the end of his seizure.

Cephas opened his eyes. Blinding pain. He closed them again. Lightning flashed inside his head, thundering against the confinement of his skull. Tears streamed down his cheeks. He squenched his eyes closed, and then opened one, slid from his chair, and crawled to the pallet.

Evelyn moved to the corner and knelt beside the writhing child. His body jerked and twitched. She wondered if he were in convulsion. "Cephas?" she said. "Cephas?" She touched his shoulder, but the boy drew back as though she'd hit him. "Are you okay, Cephas?"

"Later," he mumbled.

Evelyn returned to teaching, but she watched Cephas. Not long before dismissal, he returned to his seat and began working on the morning assignment. When the others left, he handed his paper to Teacher Lady and said, "I'm gonna bring you some crabs this afternoon. I'll bring 'em to your house." He left smiling.

Cephas was sitting on her step when Evelyn arrived. "You need to get some water boilin' afore they start to die," he said, following her into the house. She put on a pot of water and offered Cephas a fudgesicle. They sat together at her tiny kitchen table, each savoring the cold chocolate, waiting for the water to boil.

"Have you ever been to a doctor, Cephas?"

"Ain't never been off this island." He finished his popsicle and looked longingly at hers. She got him another.

"There are medicines that might help you not have seizures."

"Have what?" he asked from behind the fudgesicle.

"Your spells."

"My fits? My ma don't believe in store-bought medicine. I've always had them fits. Ever since I was born. That's why I'm a retard."

"Cephas, you're not retarded. You don't know all your school work because you miss some of the lessons."

"I been a retard all my life. Born a retard on Surcie Island, gonna die a retard on Surcie Island. That's what my ma says." He turned toward the stove. "Look! Water's boilin'!"

The boy jumped up and opened the box full of scrambling and scratching blue-shelled crabs. "You know how to cook 'em, Teacher Lady?"

"I may have a recipe for deviled crab in one of my books."

"Well, you gotta cook 'em afore you can make somethin' fancy with 'em. Get me your tongs."

The teacher watched as the child dropped the struggling creatures one by one into the boiling water.

"See 'em turnin' red?" Cephas asked. "Just like lobsters."

"Do you catch lobsters, too?" Teacher Lady said.

"No," the boy laughed. "Don't you know nothin'? Ain't no lobsters off this coast. Water's not cold enough. Lobsters is mighty tasty, but you gotta go up North to get lobsters."

"See, Cephas, today you're teaching the teacher."

"Ain't that somethin'? The retard teachin' the teacher. What we gonna do with these crabs when they get cooked?"

"How do you like them prepared?"

"I just pick the good meat out and eat it. Bet you don't even know what parts is good and what parts is bad for you."

"No, I don't."

"I'll show you."

They sat across from one another at the small table, the gray-haired teacher and the small blond boy. "Cephas," Evelyn asked, "do you have lots of spells at home?"

"Not no more. Used to do it evertime Ma took the strap to me, so now she don't beat me no more." He laughed.

"Do you think she'd let me take you to a doctor?" Evelyn asked quietly.

"Naw, my ma don't want me off this island. Mr. Kelly had a lady go talk to her. Ma says she don't want nobody messin' with me. They'd put me in one of them places for retards." He looked at her a moment, puzzled expression turning into a warm, friendly smile. "If them fits bothers you so much, I'll try not to do it so often."

They ate in silence. The woman worried about the child, trapped by his environment, yet so sweet to think he could eliminate or decrease his seizures without medical help.

Evelyn's thoughts drifted back to the present. She wondered where the child in the film was now. Probably about sixty years old, unaware of the role he'd played in the mystery of the assassination. Evelyn would have given her every possession to know what actually happened November 22, 1963. She didn't believe the American public would ever know the facts. "The positive proof just doesn't exist regardless of how much computers enhance film," she whispered to herself.

One thing she knew. Every year of her teaching, she'd tried to impress her students with how it felt that horrible day when, just a college student herself, she'd learned Kennedy was dead. Throughout her teaching career, when Evelyn Hillshire was in a classroom on the twenty-second day of November, she taught what Americans had said and done when the newsmen interrupted their lives with the fact that John F. Kennedy had been shot in Dallas.

* * *

Evelyn didn't specifically remember teaching the children of Surcie Island about Kennedy, but Cephas remembered that day well. She'd said that it was history to them, but it was personal to her.

Cephas had tried hard to listen and not get bored. It was now too cold to catch crabs. He didn't need to escape the classroom to be on the creek at the right time for the tides. Besides, Teacher Lady had been so nice to him that he hated to upset her by having a fit.

Teacher Lady made the President sound so wonderful that one of the girls cried. Cephas was captivated by the story. He knew that what he planned to do would upset her, but he'd been so good about not doing it since the day they'd eaten the crabs, and he wanted to do it so bad.

"Where did you say they shot him?" Cephas asked.

"In the head," the teacher answered.

"No, what town was he in?"

"It happened at a place called Dealey Plaza in a city called Dallas in the state of Texas."

"When?"

"About lunchtime on November 22, 1963. That's forty years ago, before your parents were born," Evelyn answered. Her delight in his interest showed on her face.

Temptation was too great. Cephas knew he shouldn't, but he just had to. He closed his eyes. *Dealey Plaza*, he thought. *In a city called Dallas. The parade. Lunchtime. November 22, 1963. Dallas in a state called Texas.*

The excitement was almost more than Cephas could bear. Throngs of people. He'd never seen anything like it. He nudged forward, hoping to get a better view.

"Here, little boy," a bearded old man said. "Move up here so you can see the President when he passes by. He'll be here soon."

The child in the faded red shirt stepped to the front. Another man with a home movie camera spotted him. He'd been panning the grassy knoll across the way, but the boy's look of total, complete involvement caught his attention. Excellent human interest shot. He zoomed the lens in on the child's face, catching forever that look of thrilled expectation.

At that moment—a noise. Confusion. The camera man turned down the street to the approaching limousine. Something was happening. The President fell over.

Cephas saw the man in the car, the one Teacher Lady liked so much. He saw the beautiful woman beside him, red on her pink dress.

He wished he'd never come. He closed his eyes and thought, *Classroom. Surcie Island. Now.* The last thing Cephas did in Dallas was put his hands to his head in preparation for the storm that would rage within him when he lifted his head from his desk.

* * *

Evelyn pressed the power button on the remote and turned off the television. She regretted watching the film. The end of November always depressed her, and all of the hullabaloo about this fifty-year anniversary made it worse. Seeing the child who reminded her of Cephas was even more upsetting. Cephas had helped her pack when Mr. Kelly returned. The boy had actually leaned through the car window and kissed her on the cheek just before she drove away.

She'd vowed at that moment to *do something* for Cephas, but, somehow, she'd never decided what she could do. The boy would be about twenty years old now. Tears filled her eyes as she thought of Cephas — the tragedy of the boy trapped by his environment, the backwardness, the ignorance. She thought Cephas was probably right the afternoon he told her he was "born on Surcie Island and will die on Surcie Island."

No, Cephas would never escape.

ONE RING

THE FIRST TIME Mom and Dad took us to spend the weekend with Mee Maw without them, my brother, sister, and I were a little scared. We lived in the city—downtown Charleston—and our Mee Maw lived way out in the country near a little town in the South Carolina midlands. We were used to city sounds after dark, but when we'd spent the night at Mee Maw's house with our parents, we'd heard strange sounds *inside* as well as animal noises outside. Besides, the trees were tall and dark around Mee Maw's house.

"It's been too long since you've visited Mee Maw," Mom said as Dad drove. "And you're definitely old enough to spend the night with your own grandparent without Dad and me staying, too."

"Why doesn't she just come to our house for the weekend?" Aeden, my twelve-year-old brother asked.

149

He had insisted that he was old enough to look after Lucille and me. Mom and Dad had flatly refused to even consider leaving the three of us without an adult in charge. We all knew Lucille would never listen to Aeden. She's the baby, nine years old, and acts like she's five. She won't listen to me either, though I'm a year older than she is and a girl. I thought I was better qualified to babysit than Aeden. Everyone knows girls are more mature than boys. That is, girls in general, not my sister Lucille.

"Mee Maw doesn't like to travel," Mom answered Aeden. "This is working out perfectly since the seminar your father and I have to attend with Mimi this weekend is in Columbia." Dad and his mother, our Charleston grandmother Mimi, frequently attended the same conventions, but Mom had always stayed home with us. Now that Mom had gone to work at the real estate office with Dad and Mimi, we were being taken to spend two nights in a house that creaked and squealed and had scary night sounds.

Don't get me wrong. Our grandmothers were very different, but we loved both of them. Mimi was slim and wore beauty parlor hair styles and sophisticated clothes. When we hugged her, we had to be careful not to wrinkle her clothes or smudge her makeup, but she loved us in her own way and took us shopping and out to lunch.

"Here we are," Dad announced as he turned into the long, tree-lined driveway up to Mee Maw's. I'd been told that there used to be a big, plantation-type house with columns at the front. It burned down before Mee Maw was born, and the family rebuilt on the same spot. Mom said the house was smaller than the original one, but it was still much larger than our home in Charleston.

Mee Maw ran out to meet us. She always did that. I asked her a long time ago how she knew exactly when we'd be there. She answered, "I always hear that big ole engine in your Daddy's car." She was wearing a red-and-white-checked dress with a blue apron over it and "old lady" lace-up shoes. Mee Maw wasn't as slim as Mimi, but she was never fat. My teacher would have called her "statuesque."

"Come right on in," Mee Maw said in her Aunt Bee voice. Our daddy liked to watch Andy Griffith in old *Mayberry* shows on television, and my brother and sister thought Aunt Bee sounded just like our Mee Maw.

We were hardly out of the car before we could smell the food. Mee Maw had cooked fried chicken, macaroni and cheese, turnip greens, cornbread, and peach cobbler. We all sat around the big oak table and enjoyed the country cooking together, but too soon, we'd finished eating. Mom said to me, "Now, Estelle, you be sure to help Mee Maw clean up the kitchen. Dad and I have to get back on the road."

Mee Maw noticed our sad faces. She said, "I have a surprise for all of you. I finally got cable television.

Guess I'll have to buy myself a computer now because they sold me a bundle, and now I'm on the Internet. My telephone is bundled, too. I never thought I'd see the day when people had a choice about what phone service to use. She grinned at Dad, and he smiled back at her. He was always doing some kind of work on his laptop.

After our parents left, we helped Mee Maw in the kitchen, and then gathered in the living room to watch television — Mee Maw in her rocking chair and the kids lined up on the couch. Through the curtains, we could see the sky darken. We were watching an old rerun of *iCarly* with Mee Maw laughing along with us when it happened.

Errrrrrrrrrrrrrrrrrrrrrrr. The loud noise from the TV introduced a weather announcement: *The National Weather Bureau has issued a severe thunderstorm warning for central South Carolina. Wind gusts may be as high as sixty miles per hour, and these storms may produce hail. Counties included are Kershaw, Lexington, Newberry, and Richland.*

Lucille jumped into Mee Maw's lap. My little sister was *still* scared of storms, and Mee Maw was a grandmama who never worried about getting her clothes wrinkled.

"Don't worry," Mee Maw said, "we have those warnings just about every evening, but it hardly ever storms here."

Just then, Mother Nature made a liar out of Mee Maw because we all heard an earsplitting crash of thunder. The wind whistled and rain pelted the roof like miniature bombs. The lights dimmed a few times, and then the house went totally dark. Aeden and I moved over closer to Mee Maw while she reached around Lucille to light a candle.

"Let's tell ghost stories," Aeden suggested.

"Not real scary ones," Lucille protested.

Aeden raised his eyebrows and twisted his mouth into a menacing face. "That's the best kind — the creepy ones."

"Yes, good ghost stories frighten everyone." I backed my brother.

"I can tell you a ghost story that isn't scary," said Mee Maw. "And it's a true story about this very house we're in right now."

"Ohhhhh, no," Lucille groaned, but Aeden and I both sat up straighter and looked right at Mee Maw.

"Tell us," my brother and I said in unison.

"A long time ago," Mee Maw said, "even before your mother was born, my sister Anne and I lived in this house. Both of our parents had already passed away. Anne was twenty-four, and I was twenty when a horrible thing happened. My sister Anne was killed in a car accident. When Anne died, some relatives stayed with me for a few days after her funeral, but then they had to go home. That night the telephone rang. It was right here in the living room where it's always been. I never could see why people need phones in every room. Guess they're just too lazy to walk to it if they're somewhere else in the house. Anyway, the phone rang, and I jumped up to answer it. When I said, 'Hello,' there was no one there even though there had only been one ring."

"It was probably a wrong number," Aeden suggested, "and the caller realized it after just one ring."

"No," Mee Maw told him, "it happened every night for weeks—usually between two and three o'clock in the morning. It was always just one ring, and there was never anyone on the line when I answered. I quit picking up the receiver, but the telephone rang only once each night for weeks. Finally it stopped."

"Oh, pshaw." Aeden frowned. "That's not a ghost story."

"I haven't finished," Mee Maw said. She looked down at my little sister in her lap. Lucille was snoring softly. "Maybe that's better," Mee Maw whispered. "I think of this as a non-scary story, but it might frighten Lucille."

"Tell us the rest." I leaned closer to her. I didn't really believe in ghosts, but I wanted to hear everything.

"Remember I told you this is about a good ghost, not scary," Mee Maw reminded. "After several months, the one-rings in the middle of the night stopped, and I didn't think much more about it. I met your Paw Paw and started dating him though thoughts of Anne still made me sad."

"Is that all?" Aeden asked.

"Be quiet," I scolded him. "She hasn't told us about the ghost yet."

"Anyway," Mee Maw continued, "after we were married, your Paw Paw took me to visit his relatives in Georgia. He had a great-aunt named Minnie who looked about a hundred years old. Paw Paw said she had the 'sight.' Aunt Minnie told me that sometimes when a person dies and didn't get to say their goodbyes to someone they loved, they send messages. These messages are called 'manifestations.' According to Aunt Minnie, the message might be sent as coins the person finds somewhere special and unexpected after a loved one dies. Another kind of message is that the survivor sees the same bird over and over."

"Is that bird the ghost?" asked Aeden.

"No, it's just a symbol." Mee Maw wiped her eyes again. "Then Aunt Minnie said that sometimes the message is sent by the telephone ringing just once during the night. When I told her about my one-rings, she said, 'It was your sister. She was letting you know she's okay.'" Mee Maw coughed. "See? I was visited by my sister's ghost, and it wasn't scary. It was a good thing—Anne letting me know she was all right."

After that, I carried the candle to the "girls'" bedroom and Mee Maw followed me, carrying Lucille. The house had lots of bedrooms, but Mee Maw had closed off all except two of them. Said it saved on heating and air conditioning bills. Aeden would sleep on the couch in the living room. Mee Maw tucked Lucille and me under the covers after I snuggled close to my sister.

The storm stopped for a while, then started up again with the wind moaning through the trees and lightning crackling outside, lighting up the inside of the house much better than the candle had. I finally went to sleep and was having a terrifying nightmare about dead people and ghosts when Mee Maw shook me.

"Wake up! Wake up!" Mee Maw screamed as she grabbed Lucille, who began squalling and crying. "We have to get out of the house. It's on fire!"

We ran outside where Aeden was standing way down the driveway calling 911 on his cell phone. When the sheriff and the fire truck got there, I was glad we'd all gone to bed in our day clothes. I didn't want those people to see me in my pajamas.

Mom and Dad came, picked us up, and carried all of us to Columbia where we stayed in a big, fancy hotel—even Mee Maw. Lightning had struck a tree, then jumped over to Mee Maw's roof and set her house on fire.

The next day, Mom said to Mee Maw, "It's a miracle that you all got out in time. Aeden said the telephone ringing woke him and he yelled to you."

I thought about that a minute and then asked, "Who called him? He always sets his cell phone on vibrate when he goes to bed."

"It was on vibrate," Mee Maw agreed. "The ringing came from my house phone."

I couldn't resist asking, "Was it a one-ring?"

"No," Mee Maw replied, "it rang over and over, just as loud as could be. I heard it the whole time while we were running from the house. The strange thing is that the electricity was off and that house phone isn't like the old Bell South ones. The cable phones don't work without electrical power."

I shivered and almost said something obnoxious like, "Do you think it rang long and loud enough to wake the dead?" I didn't say it because I was afraid it might make Mee Maw cry again thinking about her sister, and I wasn't quite sure if Anne could follow Mee Maw to the hotel.

That was a few years ago. I'm a teenager now, so I suppose it's okay to confess: I was glad Mee Maw's house burned and we never went back. I'm thankful that Anne warned us about the fire, but even now, years later, the ringtone of a telephone sends shivers up my spine.

CHESSIE

"HOW CAN WE tell her? She's not even three years old yet." Thomas paced the floor, back and forth across the bedroom, as he spoke.

His wife Margaret sat brushing her hair the self-mandated one hundred strokes per night. "The child will adjust." She said, turned away from the mirror, and frowned at Thomas. "You baby her too much, and besides, it's your fault the nanny's gone." Looking at the silver-backed brush in her hand, she added, "You've made me forget how many times I've counted. I'll have to start over." She pulled the brush through her waist-length, strawberry-blonde hair and said, "One."

Thomas used to love seeing Margaret take the pins and combs from her hair and let it tumble down her back like a golden waterfall. He remembered his excitement back in 1801 when he'd first glimpsed her ankle below the long skirt. He no longer had those feelings. Margaret was his wife, mother of his child, but she wasn't the sweet person he'd believed she was when they married.

Those thoughts remained unspoken. Instead, Thomas said, "Don't you remember when Mother brought Jessica on that long buggy ride from Charleston, promising this particular nanny would know how to care for a tiny baby born far too soon? If Jessica hadn't sat by the fireside keeping Betsy warm and feeding her from an eye-dropper every hour, we would have lost her."

"Well, now you've lost her. From what that note says, the nanny won't be back."

"You know I mean we would have lost our daughter." He paused both his walking and his words. After a full minute, he asked, "Why do you always call Jessica 'the nanny' instead of her name?"

"She was hired help, Thomas, not a member of the family." Margaret stopped brushing and turned around to face her husband. "You and Mother Morgan love to tell how the nanny promised she knew what to do for such a fragile infant—keep her dry and warm, feed her tiny amounts frequently, rock her, love her, and pray. Neither of you ever mention that I was recuperating from a difficult birth while you and your mother hovered over that woman and the baby."

Thomas assumed he and Margaret would debate the problem late into the night as they usually did when a disagreement became verbal, but she simply said, "One hundred." After she placed the hairbrush on the vanity, lay down on the bed, and pulled the quilt up to her chin, she turned her back to him, and soon began snoring. Thomas lay down beside her, but his thoughts remained on their sleeping daughter — unaware that her life would be different when she awoke.

Still delicate, Betsy loved to frolic with Jessica in the field of wild flowers beside the road leading to their home. Jessica always watched her carefully. Across the road was a wooded section, and beyond that lay the swamp.

Thomas smiled as he remembered watching tiny Betsy pick flower bouquets for her nanny and her mother. Jessica always acted as though those wild flowers were exotic blossoms from some far-away land. Margaret said, "Thanks," and handed hers to the cook to put into water in vases that somehow never found their way out of the kitchen.

At night, Thomas liked to tiptoe into Betsy's room and stand beside Jessica watching the child sleep. Sometimes he touched the soft curls on his daughter's forehead and thanked God this beautiful little girl had survived. He frequently told Margaret, "Betsy looks like an angel when she sleeps. I can understand why Jessica likes to watch her. Why don't you come to the nursery with me?"

Margaret's response was always some excuse. She was busy reading a book or writing letters to her relatives. When Thomas spoke to his mother about Margaret's lack of interest in Betsy, she told him, "Some ladies leave child-care responsibilities to their nannies but still shower love on their children. Others aren't cut out to be mothers. Just be thankful you're a planter who can afford people to run the house and a nanny who loves your daughter."

Maybe what's happened will make Margaret more loving toward Betsy, Thomas thought, but he knew that was a dream of his that wouldn't come true. Earlier this very evening, Betsy had cried, "Chessie, Chessie," which was how she pronounced "Jessica." Thomas was surprised when he went to check with Jessica to see if Betsy was sick. The nanny wasn't in the room, and Betsy was asleep. He was even more surprised when he found a note on the rocking chair by Betsy's crib. Thomas had picked the paper up from the bedside table and read:

I'm sure you both realize I can't
stay here after what happened. I
can't stand to tell Betsy I'm leaving.
Please let her know I won't be back.

Jessica

Thomas had kept the note and now he read it again. After a few minutes, Margaret rolled over and reached for it. She frowned. "If you two had behaved, none of this would have happened."

"I take my vows seriously," Thomas said. "I'd never do that to Betsy. The only thing between Jessica and me was our love and concern for Betsy. Our daughter is still not strong."

"What about me? You're only faithful, *if* you are, because of the child? You'd betray me if we didn't have her?"

"No, that's not what I meant. You're twisting things like you did during your screaming fit when you came into my office while Jessica and I were talking." He couldn't help scowling at her. "We were only discussing Betsy."

"Any decent woman would have acted exactly as I did."

"I think not. I believe most women would have listened before calling the nanny those names you used. I didn't know you even knew such words. I swear to you that nothing has happened or would ever have happened between Jessica and me."

"It doesn't matter. She's gone now, and we'll just have to find another nanny for Betsy—an ugly, old nanny."

"The bond between Jessica and me was simply that we both love Betsy. You don't believe that, do you?"

"No!" If she'd been standing, Margaret would have stamped her foot—an action as common as fainting among some Southern ladies. "We don't have to talk about that right now," she continued. "When Betsy wakes up in the morning, what are you going to tell her about her beloved Chessie leaving her for good—abandoning her?" Margaret glared at Thomas, but there was almost a smirk in her expression.

"You know perfectly well this will hurt Betsy. You almost sound happy about it."

"Don't be ridiculous. I would never intentionally do something to hurt any child." The smirk became more noticeable.

When Betsy woke the next morning, she called for her Chessie. Thomas went to the nursery and told her, "Jessica had to go bye-bye. She went on a long trip, but she wants you to be a good girl until she comes back."

Betsy nodded and answered, "I be good girl."

They got through that first day with Thomas neglecting his responsibilities so that he could take care of Betsy. She cried for Jessica several times, and during her nap, he heard her whimpering, "Chessie, Chessie." Margaret spent the day embroidering linen napkins.

During the following weeks, Thomas hoped Jessica would return and Margaret would be reasonable, but he didn't believe there was any chance of that. No matter how much Jessica loved Betsy, no decent woman would come back to be demeaned and falsely insulted by Margaret. He put Jessica out of his mind and concentrated on what to do for Betsy. She hardly ever smiled anymore, and when she did feel like playing, she wanted to be outside in the field of wild flowers. She didn't pick bouquets. Instead, she repeatedly tried to go across the road and into the woods toward the swamp.

Thomas didn't dare let anyone other than himself take Betsy outside. Many men came to the house to handle business with him now that he spent most of his business days caring for Betsy. He was haunted with worries. What if Betsy ran out in front of one of the carriages? One of the horses could trample her or she might be run over by the carriage wheels. What if she got lost in the woods on the other side of the drive? What if she wandered through the woods to the swamp?

The cook asked Thomas what he planned to do. He confessed, "I don't know."

When Thomas tried to discuss the problem with his wife, Margaret said, "The child will get over it. You and Jessica caused it."

Thomas no longer responded to Margaret when she made remarks like that. Instead, he took Betsy outside to play. At first, he was surprised when Margaret followed them. He soon realized that she was only there to continue her harping and accusations.

"Margaret, we need to watch Betsy," he tried to warn her. "Fletcher Johnson is bringing some contracts over here, and you know how that boy of his drives those horses."

"It's *your* precious Betsy who needs watching, and until you hire someone to replace Jessica, it's your job to watch her."

"*Replace Jessica?* There is no way." Thomas seated himself in one of the rocking chairs.

"Jessica, Jessica, Jessica. Your obsession with her is why she's gone," Margaret snapped.

The sound of horse hooves pounding on the earth made both of them look up just as Fletcher Johnson's carriage came racing around the curve in a cloud of dust right at the moment little Betsy stepped directly into its path.

Thomas jumped up and over the porch railing, sprinting toward his child, but in his heart, he knew he wouldn't make it in time.

When Betsy flew through the air and landed gently on the woods side of the drive, Thomas at first thought one of the horses had stepped on her and thrown her aside. A moment later he realized what he'd really seen.

His tiny daughter had been snatched from under the horses by ghostly arms that set her safely by the road.

"Her ghost! Jessica's ghost. I saw her," Margaret screamed as she ran toward her husband. "Protect me."

Thomas grabbed Betsy up in his arms as Fletcher and his driver hurried from the stopped carriage.

"Where did she go?" Fletcher questioned.

"She's right here. I've got her," Thomas answered while he patted Betsy's back.

"No, the woman," Fletcher said, "the woman who saved her."

Thomas continued comforting Betsy as she cried, "Chessie, Chessie."

"It was Jessica's ghost," Margaret said, terror all over her face. "Save me."

"Ghost?" Thomas said. "Nannies who go back to Charleston don't leave their ghosts behind."

"Chessie, Chessie," Betsy said reaching toward the woods.

Later, Thomas realized he shouldn't have said the following words in front of Betsy, but they just popped out. "She didn't go back to Charleston, did she?"

Margaret didn't answer. She sobbed and her entire body shook.

"Jessica is in the swamp, isn't she, Margaret?" Thomas's face and tone were as stern as the preacher's on Sunday mornings. "You killed and put her there. I'm going to search every inch of that ground until I find her, and then you'll answer to the sheriff."

THE SALMON STORY

"WHERE ARE THE SALMON BALLS?" Rusty questioned his mother one Sunday morning when he went to the table and found only grits, eggs, and biscuits for breakfast.

The time was the late forties; the location, a small town in the Piedmont region of South Carolina. World War II had ended, and the men who'd survived were back home, but unfortunately, Rusty's dad was one of the soldiers who didn't return, not even in a coffin. At twelve, the boy had lost his dad to whatever unknown end the war had brought, leaving hard times for Rusty and his mother Ginny, but they managed as well as possible under the circumstances. Mom went to work as a clerk in Mr. Everett's general store, and Rusty quit school to work the fields on Mr. Clyde's farm. Mr. Clyde gave Rusty surplus vegetables and eggs, and sometimes his wife sent a pie or cake home with the boy. Rusty appreciated everything, but, best of all, each Saturday night when his mama left the store, her boss said, "Virginia, take this for you and your kid," and handed her a small tin of salmon.

Every Sunday morning, Ginny cooked a big breakfast with grits, eggs, salmon, and biscuits. The biscuits were homemade, the only kind Rusty had ever eaten. There were no McDonald's, Hardees, or BoJangles in South Carolina in those days, and Rusty's family had never frequented the small diner on Main Street at breakfast time. Ginny cooked their eggs to order. She preferred hers scrambled while Rusty liked his fried hard just like Dad had eaten them.

On his plate this morning, Rusty saw two hard-fried eggs, two biscuits, and a large serving of grits. No salmon. Grits, eggs, and biscuits made a good enough breakfast, but the *piece de résistance* for Rusty was the salmon every Sunday. Ginny mixed a little chopped onion, a bit of seasonings, an egg, and crumbs with the salmon, rolled the mixture into little balls, then pressed the spheres into patties and fried them to a crisp, golden brown. In later years, Rusty would discover these were called salmon croquettes, but, to Rusty, they were salmon balls.

"Did Mr. Everett forget to give you salmon this week?" Rusty asked his mother before she had time to respond to his first question

"No, he didn't forget. It's our turn to have the preacher eat dinner with us, and since the groceries are a little short, I'm saving the salmon for lunch."

After church, Pastor Mark followed Rusty and Ginny home where they sat at the little kitchen table eating salmon balls and biscuits with vegetables instead of with grits and eggs.

"This is a real treat," Pastor Mark commented. "Most people fry a chicken when I come to dinner. Since the War, the only foods on tables in the South are directly from our farms. When fish is available, it comes from one of the local ponds or the river. I really appreciate this fine salmon. Did it come in a can?"

"Yes," Ginny replied, "it came tinned from Everett's Store."

Rusty choked back a laugh. Pastor Mark should know the only way to have salmon in their little town was from a can. The Piedmont wasn't on the coast, and even if it had been, salmon wasn't found in those warm waters of the Atlantic that bordered South Carolina.

They were eating Ginny's delicious apple pie when Rusty turned to the preacher.

"Pastor Mark," the boy asked, "do you believe in ghosts?"

"I'm not quite sure, but I know I believe in The Holy Ghost," was the answer.

"Why do you ask that?" Ginny questioned her son.

"I was thinking that if there really is such a thing as a ghost, maybe one day I'll see Dad again." Rusty wiped tears from his eyes as he spoke.

Ginny leaned across the table and patted his hand. "Honey," she said, "we don't know definitely that your father is dead, but I'm sure that if he *has* passed away and it's possible to appear to you, he will."

"I believe that, too," Pastor Mark said and took the last salmon ball and biscuit. This action made Rusty even sadder. He'd been thinking that left-over salmon ball would be mighty tasty tucked into the cold biscuit for supper that night.

"You know," Pastor Mark said as he chewed, "like I said, most folks fry a chicken when I'm coming for Sunday dinner, but I do believe these fish cakes and biscuits are the best thing I've eaten in years."

"Why, thank you, Pastor," Ginny said with a big smile. "They're Rusty's favorites, too."

Rusty was cleaning the chicken coops a few months later when Mr. Clyde came running. "Quick, Rusty," he cried out, "we've got to go straight to Everett's Store. Your mother is sick." Even though the farmer drove Rusty in his truck, they were too late. The doctor knelt by her side. Ginny had died of a heart attack.

His father gone and now his mother, too. Rusty brayed out—loud, hysterical sobs. Back at the farm, Mrs. Clyde hugged him to her, rocked him in her arms, and tried to comfort him, but nothing calmed Rusty's grief nor eased his pain. Ginny's sister Georgia came down from North Carolina and saw to the burial. Rusty went through the motions, even throwing the first handful of dirt into the grave, but it was obvious to everyone that the child was numb.

There was no talk of sending Rusty to a children's home or finding him foster parents. Child protective services were far less active in those days, and the government wasn't involved in what would happen to Rusty. Aunt Georgia urged him to go home with her to Shelby, North Carolina, but Rusty didn't want to leave. He wound up accepting Mr. and Mrs. Clyde's offer to remain working on the farm and take his meals with the family. The Clydes didn't have space for Rusty in the house, and they didn't adopt him, but they made a room for him in the loft of the barn. At sixteen, Rusty received a letter. In shaky handwriting, it read:

> Dear Russell,
>
> I'm getting old and want to see you again. My arthritis is too bad for me to travel, so I'm sending you round-trip bus fare.
>
> Love, Aunt Georgia

A week later, Mr. Clyde drove Rusty to the Columbia Bus Station. The trip was a real adventure for Rusty. He had assumed those big Greyhound buses stopped only at terminals, but the driver stopped often to pick up passengers and let others off at crossroads and filling stations. People entertained themselves reading, talking, or sleeping. There were no earbuds or MP3 players in those days.

When Rusty stepped off the bus in Shelby, he looked around for Aunt Georgia, but he didn't see her. He was getting mighty worried when an old man wearing overalls spoke to him.

"Are you Miss Georgia's nephew Russell?" the man asked.

"Yes, sir."

"I'm Walter. I work for Miss Georgia, and she sent me to get you. Come on."

Carrying the small suitcase Mrs. Clyde had loaned him, Rusty followed Walter out of the terminal to the parking lot where they climbed into an ancient Ford pickup and began the trip on bumpy, dirt roads to Aunt Georgia's house. Dust blew in the windows, but it was too hot to roll them up.

Walter turned off the road onto a long driveway that ended at a tiny, white asbestos-shingled house. A circle driveway surrounded the building and small, swept yard. There were some bushes, but no grass, and Rusty could see broom marks on the dirt. The truck stopped between the house and the barn in the backyard where Aunt Georgia met them with a big hug for Rusty. She was older, shorter, and chubbier than Ginny had been, but she still reminded him of his mother. She showed Rusty where to put his suitcase and then led him to the kitchen for supper.

Sitting at the table, Aunt Georgia made sure Rusty piled his plate high with chicken and dumplings.

"There's apple pie for dessert," she told him. "Your mother told me that was your favorite."

"Yes, ma'am."

After eating, they sat in the living room, and Aunt Georgia talked about how things were when she and Ginny were children. Then she asked, "Did you ever hear anything more from the Army about your father? Was he killed or is he still missing in action?"

"No, ma'am. I don't think we ever heard anything for sure."

"Why don't you ask your mother?"

Rusty had heard of senility—that time when old folks get confused and forget things. He figured Aunt Georgia must have a touch of that, so he gently reminded her, "Mama's dead, Aunt Georgia, remember?"

"Of course, I remember, boy! You think I'd forget my own sister died?" She paused, then added, "Have you seen her lately?"

"I told you Mama's dead."

"I see her all the time. Matter of fact, she's standing over there in the corner smiling at you right now. You ought to talk to her."

Rusty stared in the direction Aunt Georgia was pointing, but he saw nothing.

After a long evening of his aunt telling how she saw all of their dead kin folk and had conversations with them frequently, Rusty decided to shorten his stay.

"Aunt Georgia," he said, "it's been real good visiting with you, but Mr. Clyde decided he can't spare me but a day or so. I need to go back to South Carolina in the morning."

"Oh, no! I wish you'd be here longer, but when Walter comes by before he goes home, I'll tell him to pick you up early tomorrow. It's been wonderful seeing you. I'm going to tell Virginia how impressed I am with her strapping young son."

Rusty soon claimed to be tired and went to bed, but he hardly slept at all. He was too upset about the things Aunt Georgia had said. It seemed he'd barely drifted off when she called him, "Get up, Russell. Breakfast is ready!"

Her voice interrupted his sleep, but what brought him wide awake was the smell. He knew that odor, and while some people might not appreciate the fragrance of salmon, that scent was sweeter than flowers to Rusty. He pulled on his clothes and went to the kitchen, but he'd barely taken in the sight of the platter of high, flaky biscuits and golden brown salmon balls when the back door opened.

"Come on," Walter said. "I checked the bus schedule. We gotta get going."

Seeing the disappointment on his face, Aunt Georgia grabbed a brown paper bag off the counter and dropped the biscuits and salmon balls into it. "Get your suitcase, boy. You can take these on the bus with you."

Several times during the long ride home, Rusty considered opening that sack. Other people on the bus had brought their own food, but they were eating cold fried chicken or ham sandwiches made on store-bought bread. Rusty could smell the slightly fishy scent of the salmon balls through the bag, and he thought about the odor being stronger if he took them out. This embarrassed him more than the hunger in his stomach taunted him.

All the way home, Rusty fantasized about getting back to his room over the barn at the Clydes' farm and eating his salmon balls and biscuits. When the bus pulled into the terminal, Rusty couldn't stop grinning. He was starving, but he had his favorite food right there in that little brown paper sack, though the grease had soaked through the bottom of the bag. That could have been why the salmon balls smelled stronger now.

Clutching his suitcase in one hand and the bag of food in the other, Rusty followed the line of passengers down the aisle of the bus to the front door beside the driver. As he took the first step down, Rusty looked forward, and there they stood at the bottom of the steps.

His mother and father! Standing side by side, they held hands and smiled.

Maybe the grease in the bottom of the sack caused it to burst open or perhaps seeing his mom and dad shocked Rusty so much that he dropped the bag. Regardless of the cause, it fell to the floor. Biscuits and salmon balls rolled in all directions. Rusty scrambled to pick them up, but other passengers stepped on them. He looked again where Mama and Daddy had been. They were no longer there.

Rusty has eaten lots of salmon since that day more than sixty years ago—sometimes as croquettes, sometimes in a mousse or paté, and sometimes grilled and topped with fancy sauces. He's eaten salmon fresh and smoked. He's even eaten it raw in sushi. Whenever he eats salmon, Rusty thinks of his parents. He looks around in case they appear, but he hasn't seen them since that day at the bus station. He tells this story to anyone at the nursing home who will listen to "The Salmon Story," though he always adds, "I believe in ghosts, and I believe in The Holy Ghost, and one day soon I'll see my mama and daddy again."

AN ADDED TOUCH

"PENNY-PINCHER, skin-flint, tight-wad."

Those are some of the less offensive names my family and friends call me, but my cheap ways have let me save a ton of cash.

"Edgar," my wife Mary Anne nags me all the time, "with five kids, we need a bigger house." She has no idea how much money I have stashed away, but she knows we could live better than we do in the little house we've been in since we first married.

"It was hard enough when the children were little, but now that they're teenagers, it's ridiculous to stay in this place," she grumbles.

"Do you have any idea how much houses cost these days?" I snap at her and leave the house before we're in a full-fledged ruckus.

Don't get me wrong. I'm the boss of my home. You might catch me wearing a wife-beater shirt, but I've never raised my hand at a woman, and I never will. Sometimes it's best just to get away.

Sure, we still buy the kids' clothes from good will shops, and we eat the same foods we did from the beginning. A typical supper at our house might be grits and gravy made with chopped bits of fried bologna — the cheap, ninety-nine cents a pack kind. Mary Anne thinks I can afford better now since I opened my second thrift store, but living like this is how I piled up my savings.

Anyway, this time when Mary Anne lights into me about the size of our home, I stomp out of the house and down to The Crow Bar — our neighborhood refuge where it's always cool and dim. Someone (other than me) has usually fed the juke box, so there's music. These days, The Crow Bar doesn't have the odor of smoke overriding everything else, so I smell the vinegary temptation of the purple pickled eggs, sausages, and pigs' feet in the big glass jars on the bar.

Sally, the bartender doesn't seem to mind when I ask for a glass of water. I fight the urge to buy a snack, but Sally knows the big jars will win.

"Sally, can I get an egg?" I call to her.

"It would be better with a beer than that water," a voice says from behind me. I turn and see one of my nephews bellying up to the bar. He pulls a stool over beside mine and sits down. "Hey, Larry, long time no see," I say to him.

He nods at me but doesn't utter a word until after Sally slides a Miller over his way. He takes a long pull and then turns his stool to face me.

"Uncle Edgar, I am flat-out glad to see you. Got a deal that you won't be able to resist."

"I'm not loaning you any money, Larry. You know how I feel about mixing kin and cash."

"Naw, I don't need to borrow anything. I'm offering you a bargain — a real sweet deal. I'm selling my friend's house."

Before I can answer, Sally brings me a draft beer and says, "Happy Hour has begun."

I take a few slow sips, savoring the taste. Even at Happy Hour prices, one is my limit. Larry drains his bottle and motions to Sally for another.

"I'm not in the market to buy any property," I say.

Larry laughs. "You're not telling me Aunt Mary Anne's done stopped bitchin' about your little house?"

That ruffles my feathers. I blurt, "Don't ever use that word talking about my wife," and jump to my feet.

"I didn't call Aunt Mary Anne a bitch. I just meant she complains — a lot, but I apologize anyway."

I plunk my butt back on the edge of my stool as acceptance of his apology and say, "Okay, tell me about this bargain deal. How much profit is in it?"

"Well, one of my friends, a contractor, left town. He's was living in a brand-new house outside of Beaufort. Fully furnished with four bedrooms."

"That sounds nice, but I'm not interested in spending that kind of money without a great return. Houses cost too much."

"That's the sweet part of the deal, Uncle Edgar. You'd only pay three thousand dollars and take up the payments."

"Bet the payments are sky high."

"No, my friend owns the construction company. He financed only a little of the cost."

Larry picks up a bar napkin and pulls a pencil from where he had tucked it above his ear. He writes an unbelievable low number and sets it in front of me.

"And," Larry boasts, "that includes taxes and insurance."

"Real estate is too risky. I don't wanna have even that monthly payment and maybe wind up stuck with a house that doesn't sell."

"Uncle Edgar, you don't need that house as a financial investment. You should buy it to get Aunt Mary Anne off your back. You two would have the master bedroom with two walk-in closets almost big as your whole house is now. There's three more bedrooms so Harry would have his own and you'd only have two girls in each of the others instead of all those bunk beds. It's got a formal living room and dining room and a big family room with a fireplace."

"If it's such a good deal, why don't you buy it yourself?" I ask.

"I already did, but you know me and my old lady split up every month or so. We spent a few nights there and now she's gone again. With no kids, I don't need a big house like that anyway."

Larry finished his second beer. "If you wanna see it, we can ride over there right now."

Fully expecting this house to be sitting in the middle of a marsh or swamp, I'm surprised when Larry drives through the entrance of one of the newest, most exclusive neighborhoods around.

"Come on," Larry says when he parks in front of a huge beige brick house. "Let's go in through the back. You gotta see this!"

We walk through the gate and to the back of the house past an in-ground swimming pool with patio tables and beach chairs set up around it. Larry unlocks the door, and we go into what I call a den, but he says, "Check out the family room and this oversized fireplace."

A granite hearth surrounds it and a large arrangement of artificial yellow roses that look real centers the mantel. The big, cushy furniture faces a tremendous TV mounted on the wall like they do televisions in motels.

I see the kitchen across a bar with four stools on each side of it at the end of the den. Fancy canisters and small, expensive appliances that Mary Anne has mentioned wanting sit precisely on granite countertops. Larry pulls out kitchen drawers and holds up fancy silverware. He opens cabinet doors and points to dishes and pots.

"It all stays, Uncle Edgar. This place is ready to move in. Everything stays. All you have to do is go pick up Aunt Mary Anne and the kids. The beds are made and there's towels hanging in the bathrooms with matching extras in the linen closets."

Larry races from room to room, showing me the little decorator touches that I know will please Mary Anne. On the wall above the brocade couch in the living room, turquoise candles in gold sconces add a fancy touch that I know Mary Anne will love. She always wanted some of them sconces.

The master bedroom has something *I've* always wanted — a king-size bed.

By the time Larry and I go to the bank and I give him the three thousand and he signs the deed, it's after supper time. My four daughters — Susie, Ellen, Jean, and Ruthie — are all home. My oldest child, son Harry, is at work. The girls squeal with shock and excitement when I tell them, "Grab what you need to spend the night. I bought us a bigger house."

Teenaged girls squeal a lot, so I expect it from them, but even Mary Anne can't be quiet when we pull up to our new house. I use the remote Larry gave me and raise the door of the two-car garage.

Me and Larry didn't look in the garage earlier, and I'm surprised to see the side walls of the giant space are lined with pots of fake flowers. "What's with all this?" Mary Anne asks and waves toward them.

"The previous owners left everything in the house. Maybe they ran a florist," I says.

Mary Anne and our girls run from room to room happier about the house than I've ever seen them — even on Christmas morning. When I go to pick my son up from his job at McDonald's, my wife and daughters are still exploring and laughing.

It's all I can do to get everyone to go to bed before midnight, and I won't go into detail, but that night I find out just how sweet Mary Anne can be when she's feeling thankful.

Next morning we go pick up the rest of our clothes and personal items. Then I take the girls to enroll them in the middle school and high school in our new neighborhood. The next day I put our old house on the market. If I'd known how pleased that big fancy house would make my family, might would of bought something before. Then again, probably not. When you grow up poor, it's mighty satisfying to have money socked away whether you keep it in the bank or hidden somewhere else.

The girls love the pool and invite their new friends over after school often. The only complaints come from Mary Anne and Harry.

My wife's never been persnickety before, but now that we're in this fancy house, she's mighty particular.

"Edgar, you've got to stop putting those yellow roses back on the mantel," she says. "I don't like them."

"I never touched the flowers," I tell her.

"I moved 'em to the garage and put the pot of red silk tulips up there, but somebody keeps putting the roses back."

"Must be one of the kids."

"They swear they don't move things, but I think they're teasing me. I changed those candles in the sconces in the living room to white ones, too. Put the teal ones in a drawer to use if the electricity ever goes out. This morning, the white ones are in the drawer and the old ones are back in the sconces."

"Must be one of the kids," I repeat.

Harry has other complaints. "Dad, I'm nineteen years old. Will you tell Mom to stop coming in my room and tucking me in at night?"

"I don't wait up for you anymore since you finished school," Mary Anne answers.

Ruthie speaks up, "Don't fib, Mama. At night I hear you walking down the hall to go to Harry's room. We wonder why you don't check on us, too."

"And you wake me up when you pull the covers up to my chin," Harry adds.

"You're dreaming," my wife says and changes the subject. For the first time since I walked in, she smiles. "The lady next door came over this morning. She invited me to have coffee with the neighbor women at her house tomorrow."

"Are you going?" Ellen asks her mom.

"Yes."

Mary Anne meets me at the door when I get home from work the next night. The girls are with her, all of them jabbering at me.

"Hush, hush," I tell them.

When they quiet down, Mary Anne leads us to the den. She points to the yellow roses on the mantel.

"Did one of you do that?" she demands.

"No, no," the girls say.

"I put them to the garage again less than an hour ago," Mary Anne barks.

"What's going on?" I ask. "What's wrong with you?"

"I had coffee with the neighbor ladies this morning," Mary Anne begins. "They told me why you bought this house. It wasn't like you said — just because you love me."

"And why did they say I bought it?" I ask.

"Because nobody wants to live here, so it must have been dirt cheap." Mary Anne wipes tears from her eyes. "That man built this house for his wife Catherine. She had spent years planning her dream house, but he kept putting her off, telling her he was too busy to build it for her even though he owned a successful construction company.

"Catherine developed a terminal disease around the time their only child, a son, turned thirteen. Her husband began building the exact house she'd always wanted. She was hospitalized during most of the construction, but she spent her days going through catalogs and selecting furniture, dishes, and everything else they would need in their home."

Mary Anne sniffles before she goes on, "Catherine died a few days before the house was finished. Her husband set the place up the way she wanted it, right down to the forks and spoons, and then brought her here. Her funeral visitation was held in the living room with her body on the couch under the sconces."

"That's sad," I interrupt, "but you know back in the old days wakes and visitations were held in homes. I'll even spring for a new couch if it bothers you."

"Don't you understand?" Mary Anne asks me in a tone that sounds like she thinks I'm a fool. "She's still here. The house is haunted. That's why her husband and son moved out and left everything. He was scared to take away the things she'd chosen for her dream home, and it's why the house has changed owners several times since then."

The words I say next aren't fit to speak in mixed company, much less in the presence of my daughters.

Ruthie, my youngest and, truth be told, my pet, steps closer to me and says, "Daddy, the man who lived here didn't own a florist. All those artificial plants in the garage are from his wife's funeral, and none of us are moving the yellow roses. It's Catherine's ghost."

"Ridiculous!" is the nicest word that comes from my mouth.

My family eats supper in silence, and the girls don't even tell me goodbye when a family friend picks them up to go to Youth Group.

I watch Mary Anne bend over loading plates into the dishwasher rack. Harry is at work. The girls won't be home for a couple of hours. Thinking about how sweet my wife has been since we moved, I pat her on the fanny and say, "I'm going to get me a quick shower. Hurry up with that and meet me in our room."

Soon I'm snuggled under the covers of our king-size bed. I feel a slight depression of the mattress, and soft breasts press into my back. I smile. A hand reaches around me and long, slender fingers rake through my chest hair, and then dip lower.

"If you think you're getting any more loving from me in that bed, you're sadly mistaken," my wife says.

I jump up, pull on shirt, pants, and shoes. "Get in the van," I tell Mary Anne. "We'll pick the kids up and go to a motel for the night. We're not spending another hour here."

Ever since then, when Mary Anne mentions that night, she smiles big, thinking her threat scared me so bad that we moved. What I've never told her and never will is that just as she said, "If you think you're getting any more loving from me in that bed, you're sadly mistaken," the hand sliding down my chest reached my abdomen. As I felt fingers touch me intimately, I looked up and saw my wife standing across the room in the doorway.

ROOM SERVICE

"WHEW . . . "

Amelia breathes a sigh of relief as she closes and locks the motel room door. Driving through rain and lightning has exhausted her, forcing her to stop for the night before she reaches her destination. *Damn this storm. I hate having to stay at this dump,* Amelia thinks. She throws her overnight case onto the bed, opens it, and takes out a nightgown, a bottle of Pantene shampoo, a bar of Dove soap in a zip-lock bag, and her tooth-brushing kit.

None of those generics in their plain white and black wrappers for me anymore, she thinks. *Thanks to what the reviewers call my "break-out" novel, I can afford to bring my favorite brands instead of those dinky little bottles most motels supply.* She steps into the bathroom and notices that this unexpected stop offers neither generics nor a coffee pot. The only things on the countertop are one white towel and a washcloth. She picks them up and realizes they both feel hard and scratchy. *Damn this storm,* Amelia repeats as an extended rumble of thunder penetrates the concrete-block walls of the motel.

She remembers her mother's words every time it thundered: "Don't turn the water on during a storm, Amelia. The lightning will come in along the pipes and kill you."

Since Mom's death, Amelia has learned many of those old sayings aren't true, but she decides not to take any chances. She drops her clothes to the floor, thinking, *I'll pick them up tomorrow morning,* and pulls her pink nightgown on over her head.

Back in the bedroom, Amelia shoves the overnight case to one side of the mattress and crawls beneath the covers on the other side. The sheets and pillowslips are as coarse and rough-feeling as the towel and washcloth. She reaches over to the bedside table and clicks off the light.

Damn this storm, she thinks again as she wiggles around, punching and patting the thin, lumpy pillow, trying to get comfortable, yet knowing she won't sleep until the storm ends. One spot feels especially hard. Amelia reaches under the pillow, fingers around, and then pulls out a small piece of plastic. She looks at it. A cell phone similar, but not exactly like her iPhone 6S Plus. She flips it over. Instead of the familiar Apple icon on the back, she sees the word "Futura."

Futura? That's interesting, she thinks. *I never heard of that brand.*

A flash of lightning illuminates the room for a few moments. Chill bumps pop up on Amelia's arms, and she shivers as the darkness returns. She moves from the bed to the chair beside the bedside table and turns the lamp on before she touches the home button to activate the phone.

At the password prompt, she fools around with several guesses before trying her own password—nothing. After numerous attempts, her fingers seem to have a mind of their own. As though possessed, she enters tomorrow's date. It works.

Seeking the owner's identify, Amelia touches "contacts," but there are none. Next, she tries the photo app to launch pictures. *Maybe the owner's photos will give me a clue about who owns this phone and why their password is tomorrow's date,* she tells herself, but in her heart, Amelia knows checking the pictures is a manifestation of that dominant characteristic of writers—curiosity, or to call a spade a flippin' shovel, nosiness.

The first photo brings a gasp from Amelia—a bed in a room like she's sitting in right now. The headboard is the same, but the white linens are thrown back, and a large irregularly-shaped stain dominates the left side of the once-white mattress. Some spots in the murky red blob are so dark they look black.

Another crash of thunder startles Amelia, causing her hand to jerk and unintentionally bring up the next photo—a smashed bedside table lying sideways with the legs broken off. Clearly visible scratched into the tabletop are the words: HELP ME.

Deliberately, Amelia's finger swipes over the cell phone screen, rapidly revealing pictures, one after the other. A woman in a pink nightgown, facing away from the camera, lies on the bed with her hands tied behind her back. In the next one, two plastic champagne glasses and a green bottle of cheap, gas-station wine sit beside the landline phone on the bedside table, which is upright and unbroken in this photo.

Amelia glances over at the real table beside the bed where she lay a few moments ago. She has to lean over to read them, but the letters are there—H-E-L-P-M-E—just like in the photo. Her eyes drop to the floor and she sees a thin sliver of broken green glass and a damp spot on the worn carpet.

"Damn this storm," she says aloud this time. *If not for the storm, I'd be down the road at a decent hotel.*

She considers calling 911, but what would she say? Amelia grabs the landline phone and presses O for the operator at the check-in desk. As soon as a connection is made, she begins talking. "I'm in room 120, and I've found a cell phone. I'd like someone to come get this telephone and the magnetic room key. I'm leaving." As she disconnects, she mumbles, "The hell with this damn storm." She dashes into the bathroom with the cell phone still in hand. When she reaches over to pick up her clothes, she stumbles. Sprawled on the floor, she glances down at the screen—another picture, this one obviously a selfie.

The man in the screen is wild-eyed, buck-toothed, and grinning.

Amelia hears a knock. *Damn! That was fast,* she thinks as she pulls herself up by holding onto the toilet.

She rushes to the door calling, "Who is it?"

"Room service." A masculine voice—low, steady, and pleasant.

Standing on her tiptoes, Amelia stares through the peephole. The man is looking the other way, but she can tell from his uniform that he's a motel employee, and she surmises from the haircut that he's clean-cut. She unlocks the chain latch and opens the door just as he turns toward her. In his hands are two champagne glasses, and tucked under his arm is a green bottle of cold duck.

The overhead light glistens off the man's bald head, and he grins through his buck teeth as Amelia screams and screams and screams.

AN ODOR YET TO COME

A story doesn't have to feature a ghost, monster, vampire, or other paranormal creature to leave the reader shivering with fright.

"WHAT THE HELL HAPPENED?" I open my eyes. The overnight case I'd put in the trunk of the car is smashed against my face. I'm able to slightly turn the top of my body, but when I try to straighten my legs, they won't move. Strange that they don't hurt. My heart pounds faster, and I can't think clearly. Pain screeches in my head and the world is fuzzy. Something drips down my face. I reach up, slide my hand across my forehead, and look.

It's covered with blood. I wipe my fingers on my blouse and then touch my lips. More blood.

Where am I? I was driving to my sister's house even though she suggested, "Maybe you should wait and come tomorrow. The forecast is for more storms, and these country roads aren't very good."

"No problem," I answered. "I've been driving out to your place for years, and there's no way that I'm going to miss my only niece's first birthday dinner tonight."

"Be careful at Dead Man's Curve."

"I know that road like the back of my hand."

I'd loaded my luggage and umbrella into my old hatchback and left in plenty of time to be at Cathy and Jim's long before dark. The storm eased and the rain stopped. With my favorite CD playing, I'd been singing as I approached Dead Man's Curve. My song turned to cuss words when an SUV came barreling toward me on my side of the road.

Next thing I know, I'm here with half of my body trapped under metal car parts. I attempt to move my legs, but they won't budge, and I can't feel them. I can't see them either. The front of the car is crushed and my legs disappear under where the steering wheel should be. Odd that there is no pain in them. I wrap both hands around my upper left thigh to try to lift it, straining so hard that my arm muscles scream, but my leg won't budge. Neither does the right one. Now I realize what I'm seeing—the engine of the car has been thrown back into the cab with my legs imprisoned beneath it.

The seats and console are smashed into the trunk, and my body is twisted so that my head is pressed against the luggage I had back there. I strain and look at the top few inches of my legs, barely visible before they disappear under the engine. The car must be folded like an accordion.

I remember the odor of baking pound cake. That's what I smelled right before I saw that SUV. The sweet vanilla scent of my mother's recipe. Cathy must have planned to bake one for Amber's birthday cake.

In the past few years, I've grown used to the smells. Other people might think it was coincidence when I smelled the smoky scent of steaks sizzling over charcoal before I went to my brother's. He'd told me he was cooking vegan chili, but when I arrived, I found him out back on the deck — grilling juicy ribeyes. "Hi, Megan, help me celebrate my falling off the vegan wagon," he'd greeted me.

"More like you're leaping from it," I replied.

That was the first incident.

It's not dark yet, and when I look through the broken glass of the windshield, I see wet, glistening leaves of heavy undergrowth and gigantic trees. Now I know where I am — in the deep culvert beside the curve in the road.

I listen for sirens. That SUV must have hit my car or run me off the road into the massive tree the front of my car is wedged against. Surely whoever was driving the SUV has called for an ambulance.

Just lie still. Help will come soon, I silently tell myself. I try to turn in the direction I think is toward the road, but I can't. Where are the air bags? Why didn't they deploy? Am I victim of a manufacturing defect or did the impact disable them?

Where are the police and EMTs? I can't move my legs. I need someone to lift all that metal off them. They'll probably have to use the Jaws of Life to get me out of here. Why can't I feel my legs? *It's better that way — no pain in them,* I remind myself. I'm thirsty. I feel around searching for the water bottle I'd had up front. No luck.

My mind goes back to odors. The next incident after the steaks was one day when I was shopping. Before I entered my favorite department store, I distinctly smelled something very pleasant, clean, and slightly floral. When I stopped at the perfume counter, the clerk sprayed a new sample. It was what I'd smelled outside the store. I assumed I must have passed another customer who'd tried the fragrance.

When will someone come? It's raining again and I'm getting soaked. The roof of the car is peeled back like the open lid on a can of sardines. If I could free my legs, I could just climb out the top. My thirst grows bigger and bigger. I lean my head back and catch rain in my mouth, but if I open wide, the water chokes me.

Sardines bring memories. My dad used to eat them when he went fishing, and my mom fussed about the smell. I consciously try to summon up the aroma of sardines, but my mind isn't working very well. About six months ago, I finally realized the truth about the smells. I'd been driving the same route to work every day for years until I noticed that every time I passed the house on the corner of Oak and Pine Streets, I had difficulty breathing. When I realized that I was smelling smoke and it became stronger every day, I started taking a different road. I saw that house engulfed in flames on the news a few nights later. Cathy doesn't believe me, but it's real. Oh, the perfume could be explained, but most of the scents have been predictions. I smell something and then it happens. When I told Cathy about my precognitive smells, she insisted I go to the doctor.

"Megan, I saw on the Internet that phantom smells are signs of a brain tumor," she said.

I laughed it off, but I did consult a specialist who put me through a ton of tests. The tight closeness of the MRI machine gave me the same feeling I have now—entombed by metal, unable to escape. The difference is that if I'd asked, the technicians would have let me out. There's no one here to do that.

Think about something else, I tell myself. Cathy and Jim are probably worried by now. They'll call the police and send them looking for me. My thoughts go to my little niece Amber. Only last week, I'd been holding her when I quickly handed her over to Cathy.

"She needs changing," I said. Cathy unsnapped the toddler's onesie and peeked down the back of her diaper.

"No, she doesn't." An hour later, I noticed a strained expression on Amber's face, and sure enough, she'd filled her diaper with something that smelled exactly like the scent I'd detected earlier. Cathy tried to write that one off by telling me the baby must have had gas while I was holding her, but I know better.

Why doesn't anyone come? It's raining so hard that it's impossible to swallow the water as fast as it falls into my mouth. I squench my lips together and squeeze my eyes shut.

I hear voices from a distance.

"She should be around here."

"There ain't any skid marks to show she went off the road. I don't think there's a car here. I believe that woman decided to skip the party and is in some club down town. The sister just can't accept that she wouldn't want to spend a Friday night celebrating a one-year-old's birthday."

"Don't be so cynical, but I admit you're probably right. No signs of an accident. The storms have battered down the plants and even felled some trees, but I can't see any signs that a car went off the road, no matter what the sister says."

"Yeah, you're probably right. Let's get out of here."

"No, no, no," I scream. "I'm here. Come this way." Why don't they hear me? The sounds of their voices come to me above the noise of the rain.

The wind. It's blowing toward you and bringing their shouts with it. This time is different from before when I talked to myself. The voice in my head seems to be a separate entity.

"Come back," I yell over and over as loud as I can until my voice fails.

Silence except for the wind and rain. I never realized how noisy rain is nor how cold it is even in spring time. The water sluices off my head and shoulders. My shivers turn to convulsive shakes.

Sleeping under the circumstances seems impossible, so I must have passed out. I nod my head as consciousness returns. *Where am I? What happened?* Then I remember and am aware that I'm trapped in my car. The storm is over. No rain. No wind.

I'd give anything for a bottle of water. Or even better—a cup of coffee. I recall the convenience store where I stopped for coffee a lot of mornings on the way to work. When I first began smelling something strange, I didn't know what it was. After a few times, the odor became strong enough that I recognized it— gunpowder from my childhood when my brother took me target shooting or hunting with him before he decided to become a vegetarian.

By then I knew that sometimes what I smelled predicted events to come. *About damn time!* the voice scolds me. The morning after I stopped going to that store, two coked-up kids robbed it and shot the owner.

The bottom half of my body might as well be dead. I feel nothing from the waist down, but above there, I'm hungry. I expected to be eating a big birthday dinner with cake and ice cream, so I skipped lunch. *Think about something else.*

What's happening below my waist? Have I wet myself? *It doesn't matter. When they cut you out of here, they won't know the difference between urine and rain water.*

Why doesn't someone rescue me? It's getting dark. I don't like the idea of spending the night here. *Doesn't much matter what you like.*

The moon rises—full and golden—so the sky isn't really black. I need to relax, reserve my energy until someone else comes searching for me.

I never realized how noisy the night is. I hear little scurrying sounds, some kind of small animals. What are they? Moles?

Or rats?

"God," I pray out loud, "don't let that be rats." Snakes. They slither, don't they? Would they make that sound? Doesn't matter. I pray some more, "Don't let a snake come either," and then add like I did when I prayed when was a little girl, "Please, God, please."

What's happening to my legs beneath the engine? They must be smushed, which means there's blood. Am I hearing some land animal that's attracted to the smell of blood like sharks?

Sharks are the least of your worries, Sweetie.

"Shut up!" I shriek at the voice in my head that now seems to be an entirely detached person from me.

You can't make me. You can't do anything at all but cry for help that isn't coming.

I've read about people who gnawed or cut off a limb that was hopelessly stuck.

Yes, but it would take an axe to chop off the bottom half of your body, and then you'd bleed to death, Sweetie.

My legs and belly are surely bleeding now. I can't understand how I'm still alive and alert.

Who knows? Maybe the heat of the engine cauterized the wounds. Maybe anything. No way to know until you're out of here, and Sweetie, it doesn't look like that's going to happen.

Cathy won't let them stop looking for me. She'll never give up.

What makes you so sure of that? Remember the times you stood Cathy up for lunch dates and forgot to call her?

This is different. I have more to say, but I stop. I hear something. My heart leaps to my throat. Someone is coming.

I scream again, "Help, help."

Over and over I shout that one word. I stop when I realize that the answering calls I hear aren't words. Howls. What makes that sound? A wolf? A coyote?

Doesn't matter. You'll make a delicious midnight snack for whatever it is. Maybe death will be quick. Maybe the animal will attack your throat first and you won't suffer through being slowly devoured. That will save you from wasting away from starvation and dehydration..

"Shut up! Shut up! Shut up!"

I'm yelling at the person who seems to have taken residence in my brain, but I'm amazed that the howling stops. Did I scare the animal away?

My nose itches. I reach up to scratch it, and my hand comes away with a big black spider crawling on it. I shake my hand trying to fling it off, but it doesn't move, so I pick it off with my other hand and throw it as far away as I can. I've always disliked spiders. Now I hate them as much as I do snakes.

"Hoo, hoo." The questioning sound startles me. What's that?

Don't be a fool. You know that sound. It's an owl.

I look around as far as I can and see bright round eyes above me. I can barely make out the shape of the bird perched there. It's bigger than I thought an owl would be. What if it swoops down and pecks out my eyes?

Dawn comes in silence as the bird and I stare at each other. Finally, it says, "Hoo, hoo," again. This time the noise seems almost a laugh instead of a question. I hear a slight flutter of wings as I watch the owl fly away.

Thirst. I've never been so thirsty in my life. Tears sting my eyes and suddenly I'm in a total meltdown with sobs that wrench my body – or at least the part of my body I can feel. As I weep and blubber, I stick my tongue out, trying to catch the salty liquid. I hear moans and then realize I'm listening to myself.

I smell oil.

Is this a prediction? Does the scent have any future meaning? I envision someone riding around on an ATV looking for me – an ATV with an oil leak. That illusion lasts only a few seconds before I realize that I can see oil slicked around me. This smell isn't a prediction; it's reality.

The sun takes over the sky, and the trees around me loom into focus. They provide shade, but not enough to protect me from the heat. Sweat beads on my forehead, and I can feel it under my arms. A faint, unpleasant whiff assaults my nose. BO? Am I smelling my own body odor? As the afternoon stretches endlessly, the stink becomes stronger.

Sweetie, that's not sweat you smell.

"I told you to shut up and go away," I scream at that person who has occupied my brain. Or am I shouting at myself? I don't know. I honestly don't know.

Get real. What you're smelling is decay. Just like when you went to the beach for a week and left your freezer door open. Rotted meat.

"Did the animals kill something yesterday and leave parts of their prey?" I must be going crazy because I answer the voice in my head aloud.

No. It's an odor yet to come. A smell from the future. It's you, all right, but that stench will take a few days to develop.

"Stop it!" I scream and pound the sides of my head with my hands. "Go away."

All evening I long for escape from this prison. I no longer hope for rescuers to free me and take me to a hospital and someday home. If someone came along and offered me a loaded gun, I would fly away from here on a bullet through my brain.

That rotted, decayed smell grows stronger with each passing hour. I try to talk to the person inside me, but she's not here anymore.

I don't know why, but beating my head worked. She's gone away. Now I am here alone, and I wish she would come back. I have a question for her:

"Does it hurt to die?"

A DOG NAMED DAISY

MARK HAWTHORNE was unconscious when the paramedics strapped him to a body board and removed him from the wrecked car. Only minutes before, it had been ripped open with the Jaws of Life by EMTs who'd thought the trapped man was dead.

He remained unaware of anything around him during the ambulance ride with sirens blaring and in the hospital for months. His brother Michael stood by the bed horrified at the tubes and wires protruding from Mark in all directions but always hopeful that his brother would open his eyes or move a finger — anything that showed Mark still inhabited the scarred body that used to be identical to Michael's own. As time passed, most of the tubes and wires were removed, but there was never any sign of wakefulness.

"Are you sure this is the right thing to do?"

LAUDENSLAGER, RIZER & GUESTS

Michael asked the nurse even though the doctor had assured him several times.

"Yes, Mr. Hawthorne. Your brother is breathing on his own now and with the feeding tube he doesn't need hospital care. His treatment is maintenance, and that can be handled at the skilled-care nursing facility. His condition is not classified as a permanent vegetative state, but there's a only a slim chance he'll ever wake up." She smiled at Michael, but it was a sad smile. "The ambulance will be here for him soon."

The nurse paused before adding, "And, Mr. Hawthorne, there's no need for you to continue visiting every day. He's not aware that you're here. Don't you have to go back to work?"

"I keep hoping Mark will wake up. When he does, or I guess I should say, *if* he does, I have to be here to tell him Amber didn't make it." The tall, good-looking man wiped tears from his eyes. He couldn't accept that his twin brother's wife had been killed in the car wreck that had also taken Mike's life as much as if he were in a grave instead of lying in a hospital bed while his muscular body shriveled despite the feeding tube.

Michael came every day and saw that his brother was treated kindly. The care at the skilled-care nursing facility wasn't much different from the way it had been at the hospital. When Michael was confident of that, he went back to work and only visited

Mark on weekends, so he wasn't there the Tuesday morning that Mark's condition changed.

The first wakefulness was not thought, but touch, an awareness of contact—a warm, comforting pressure against Mark's side from his waist all the way down his left leg. Vaguely reminiscent of spooning with his wife Amber, this felt different, somehow heavier.

He sank back into obscurity—the total blackness of complete unawareness.

When the darkness lifted again, Mark was aware of the position of his left arm as well as the heaviness against his side. Slowly, sensation trickled into his left hand. His fingers rested on something soft and furry, perhaps a plush throw pillow. Although he struggled to climb out of the dark depths, Mark sank into unconsciousness again.

"Some possible good news, Mr. Hawthorne," the attendant told Michael when he arrived that Saturday for his weekly visit. "One of the nurses saw your brother move the fingers of his left hand and instructed all of us to watch for motion. This could be a sign that he's coming around."

Michael stayed by Mark's bedside all day Saturday watching for any voluntary movement, but saw none. He looked around his brother's room at the many items he'd brought from Mark and Amber's house. The doctors had suggested to Michael that Mark's room at the skilled-care facility be made as familiar as possible and that Michael fill an MP3 player with Mark's favorite music to be played for the patient in hopes of stimulating him out of the coma.

Mark was alone late Sunday night when he surfaced from the nothingness. His fingers sought the luxurious feel of fur he'd learned to expect by his side. When he didn't find it, he opened his eyes — not fully, just a sliver. Even with only the nightlight, the brightness hurt. He closed them again and for the first time in months, Mark had a conscious thought: *Where am I? In a hospital?*

He forced himself to open his eyes again and look as much around the room as he could though his neck was stiff. A wall-mounted shelf to his right was probably meant for flowers, but instead someone had placed cherished items from his and Amber's home there.

Framed photographs included Mark and Michael as little boys and their parents. If Mark had been thinking clearly, he might have questioned why there were no pictures of Amber. Instead, he focused on the man's trinket case he'd made out of mahogany in high school shop class for his dad. Not the kind to wear any jewelry except his plain gold wedding band, Mark's father had cherished the polished wooden box though it stayed empty. When he passed away, his wife returned the case to Mark before she, too, died.

Tears spiked Mark's eyes, and he sought the only comfort he'd known recently. His eyes roamed the room looking until he found her.

Daisy — Amber's "fur baby" — lay sleeping on the floor beside his bed. He remembered buying the boxer puppy for Amber when their friends started having families. She had wanted a baby, but Mark preferred to wait until they were more established before having children. He bought the tiny brown puppy with four white socks for Amber, but long before Daisy reached her present almost sixty pounds, she had shown a strong preference for Mark.

He tried to call her.

"Daisy," Mark said, but his vocal cords hadn't awakened. Though no sound came out, the dog lifted her head and looked at him with dark brown eyes filled with love. She stood and shook her body slightly as she had every time she woke up since they'd brought her home only six weeks old.

She ambled over to the bed, put her front paws on the side of the mattress, and crawled up beside Mark. She wriggled into position beside him and when his fingers rubbed her back through the fur, she rolled over as she had so many times in the past. In his mind, Mark heard Amber say, "Look at her, Mark. She wants her daddy to rub her belly."

As much as Mark would have liked to talk to Daisy and stroke her forever, that minimal exertion exhausted him and after a few quick ear scratches, he fell into a deep sleep, though not back into the coma.

In the following weeks, Mark drifted in and out of vague periods of wakefulness and slight movement. Once he became aware of wet, pleasant warmth on his body and realized that someone was bathing him. He wanted to open his eyes and see if the gloved hands belonged to Amber, but instead he relaxed back into slumber.

I'm like a baby again, Mark thought. He remembered his mother used to say that when he and Michael were infants, they "got their days and nights mixed up." *Yes, a baby again,* he thought because he seemed to sleep most of the day and lie awake petting Daisy most of the night. He still hadn't found the ability to speak and let the nurses (he had determined the people who cared for him were hospital staff) know he was alive.

That thought sent Mark off into an unreasonable fear that the authorities might decide he was dead and bury him. *Ridiculous!* he silently told himself. *I'm being cared for after some kind of incident. A stroke or maybe an aneurysm, something like that. They know I'm alive or they wouldn't let Daisy stay indoors with me like a service dog. Amber must be going to work during the days when the nurses are here. Daisy always has food and water even though I never see the nurses take care of the bowls. Amber probably fills them and walks Daisy when she's home from work and by then, I'm always asleep.*

Mark was vaguely aware that Michael was there some days, but try as he might, the patient couldn't manage to speak or stay awake during the daylight hours. The only consolation for Mark's miserable existence was the constant presence of Daisy by his side or lying on the floor beside the hospital bed each night.

The dog seemed to realize the seriousness of Mark's condition and importance of his care. Whenever a nurse or attendant entered the room, the boxer slid quietly off the bed and moved to the corner of the room where she waited out-of-the-way until no one was there but her and Mark.

Michael had almost given up hoping for Mark to improve, and he wasn't surprised when the attending physician asked to see him.

The doctor was almost a foot shorter than Michael, but Michael always felt small in the older man's presence.

"To be honest with you, Mr. Hawthorne, I'm becoming more concerned about your welfare than my patient's." He spoke with the confidence and authority of his profession. "Your brother may live a very long time in his present condition. That is, unless you decide to remove the feeding tube. You do have the legal right to do that. Are you considering taking that action?"

"No, never," Michael responded.

"Then I want you to stop being here every day. Go back to work. Get a life. You can still come, but once a week is plenty. If he ever regains consciousness, yes, come like you've been doing, but until that happens, it's plenty for you to visit once a week." He smiled. "No point in ruining your own health. The time for these daily visits will be if he ever does come out of it."

Michael sat by Mark's bed late that Sunday night. He was remembering their childhoods when he heard the soft whisper.

"Daisy." The word didn't sound like his brother's strong, masculine voice, but Michael recognized it anyway.

"Mark? Mark?" Michael stood up from the chair and leaned over Mark to say his brother's name. He looked down and saw Mark's fingers moving.

"Mark, are you awake?" Michael asked.

"Michael? What happened?" Mark whispered.

"It's me, brother. You were in a car accident. You've been in a coma."

"Where's Amber?" Mark knew the answer when he looked at Michael's face. He could see the pain in his brother's eyes and felt it in the way Michael reached out and stroked his cheek.

Daisy turned her head toward Mark's hand rubbing her ears and stretched to lick his fingers.

"I'm sorry." Michael's voice caught before he

finished the statement, "Amber didn't make it."

Tears filled both brothers' eyes.

"Thank you for bringing Daisy here to be with me," Mark said. "I don't think I would have gotten through this without her by my side."

"Daisy?" Michael coughed. "I'm sorry, Mark, so sorry, but Daisy was killed in the wreck. I had her cremated. Didn't know where you'd want me to spread the ashes. They're in that container." He pointed to the mahogany box on the flower shelf.

Part Three

OUT OF THE SWAMP

GUEST AUTHORS

L. MICHELLE COX

JENIFER BOONE LYBRAND

NATHAN R. RIZER

J. MICHAEL SHELL

ROBERT D. SIMKINS

TWO RAVENS

INTRODUCTION

A COLLABORATION by Richard D. Laudenslager and Fran Rizer, *Southern Swamps and Ruins* resulted from Fran and Richard meeting in 2012 while working with other writers on a previous anthology. When the editor and publisher changed the concept of that project before contracts were issued, Laudenslager and Rizer withdrew their submissions.

Southern Swamps and Ruins became a reality when Odyssey South Publishing agreed to release it as a collection featuring fifteen stories by Laudenslager and Rizer. As the book neared completion, they invited others who had withdrawn from the previous anthology before contracts were signed to submit their narratives to be included in this collection. Part Three features a story by each of these six authors.

Into the swamp, through the swamp, and now out of the swamp. Enjoy these journeys through writers' experiences and imaginations—vivid demonstrations of Southerners' fascination with the unexplainable.

THE NET

BY L. MICHELLE COX

A STRONG WHIFF of rotten chicken hits me as soon as I begin leaning down into the back of the old car. *I really need to throw that out and start fresh,* I think to myself as I begin untangling the necessary equipment jumbled in the back of the car. I had carelessly thrown everything on the floorboard when leaving the house. The urge to go had hit me with a swift and sudden urgency, as if I had no other choice. Never mind the dishes in the kitchen sink that needed washing or the dogs that desperately needed bathing.

I shake my head as if to clear it. This is *not* why I am here. I am not here to think about things that need to be done. I am here to refresh my soul and enjoy the last days of summer warmth before it gets too cool. I am here so I don't forget. I am here to remember. Remembering is hard, but forgetting is worse. Forgetting is my greatest fear . . . a fear that leaves me paralyzed some days as I frantically search my mind for wisps of memories long past. Just a fragment of a picture in my mind. Coming here helps me to remember.

With a sigh, I begin the treacherous journey down the path to the creek. Edisto Creek they call it. I never understood that. Isn't Edisto a river? Or an island? As I get farther along, my feet begin to leave the safety of the matted grass and indent the ground beneath. The smells hit me even before my feet begin to sink dangerously into the plough mud. Memories wash over me, and I am suddenly at peace. I have been down this path before. Perhaps I am even walking in the very footsteps my sons and I took the last time we were here together. That thought steadies me as I navigate through the slimy mud, careful to avoid the sharp edges of the oyster shells that so often sliced our feet to shreds.

I never could get the oldest one to wear shoes, I remember. That boy always was a free spirit. Down deep in my gut, where everything good and bad started, I had known that he would never live long enough to get married, have children. Regret washes over me for the millionth time as I remember how many times I tried to tell him to be careful, to not drive in the rain, to be careful with that pellet gun. Worry kept us from having a close relationship, the one where you share everything and call every day just to say, "Hi." He always sighed and said, "Yes, Mama," when I scolded him out of fear. I had known I couldn't keep Fate from taking him. Why had I not been able to just let him be?

Eyeing the landscape as I made it past the bridge and down to the water's edge, I wince as I see a young mother is already there with her small son, showing him how to slowly pull in the string. Bright yellow hair frames his smiling, sweaty face as he shrieks with excitement when he sees the crab on the end of the line. His mother laughs when she realizes he has scared the crab away. My eyes blink back tears as I think how much like my son he looks.

Getting far enough away, plopping my bucket down, I look out into the murky water, seeing if I can spot the little critters myself that sometimes skirt the edge of the tide, as if daring us to step in the water. The most fun was when we could scoop them out even without using the sticks and chicken. I begin busying myself by stabbing the sticks down into the sand one by one, throwing the line out as far as it can go before pulling the stick taut. Grabbing the net, I dip it in the water before slowly pulling the first line in.

"That's not the right way, Mama," says the little yellow-haired boy that has abruptly appeared just inches from me. "Remember how we always scooped them from the top, and you said it was more fun that way?"

Frozen, I drop the net and just stare at him, not really seeing anything as tears wash away my vision.

"Mama, don't be sad," he says. "I loved that you worried about me and wanted to keep me safe. It's okay. I came back." With a furtive glance toward the woman down the beach, he continues quietly, "I chose my new mom because she's like you. I promise I will be more careful now, so she won't have to worry like you did. I'm sorry." He adds, "I love you."

With that, before I can form any words, the little boy scampers off down the sand and jumps onto his mother piggy-back style to hitch a ride up the bank. They are past the bridge and on their way to their car before I am able to mutter the words that have made their way from my grieving heart out into the still, briny air: "Thank you."

THE RUBY RING

BY JENIFER BOONE LYBRAND

Dedicated to all who are missing . . . and to the families who continue to search for them.

A BRIGHT SHARD of ruby light flickers in a slender beam of morning sun that is filtering its way through the maze of the leaves and branches in the lush canopy to the dew-dampened ground below. As the new day approaches, blue jays and sparrows sing along to the soft breeze whispering through the summer trees that cast their dappled shadows onto the creek bed below.

Hidden Creek is actually just a steady stream of tannin-stained water that flows from a deep underground natural aquifer and meanders its way across five miles of a swampy, muddy-bottomed gully until it reaches the Congaree River east of Columbia. The narrow creek runs relatively shallow in some areas, but years of steady flow have carved out a rather deep ravine that passes under several busy roadways including Shop Road and Bluff Road as it makes its way to the river's edge.

If I had to guess, it was named Hidden Creek because the flourishing oaks and pines along its banks have grown tall and full, completely hiding the creek from view, giving passersby on the bridge above the illusion the land is level below them rather than steeply sloping down thirty feet or more.

This summer has been typical for South Carolina, especially here in Columbia where I work, miserably hot and humid all day with thunderstorms rolling in late in the afternoons and evenings. Today is no different. Just minutes from quitting time and I can already hear the thunder's rumbling echo in the distance announcing its oncoming fury.

Some days it seems like all I do is fix everyone else's problems on top of someone else's mistakes and never really get a chance to sit down and complete a task start to finish. Professional Multi-Tasker should be my title instead of Administrative Assistant. Now that 4:30 is finally here, I gladly shut down my computer, grab my purse, day bag, and laptop, and lock the office door behind me as I set out for the afternoon.

Parking is at a premium on the university campus, so I have about a block and a half to walk from the office to the car, but it allows time to stretch my legs before the twenty-five-minute drive home. Looming to the east, and dark and heavy with the coming storm, the clouds are an ominous presence greeting me as I walk out of the building. I make it halfway across the parking lot when the first huge splashes of rain hit the sidewalk in front of me. I dig in my bag for an umbrella, realizing at the same moment that I have left it in the office, which triggers a monumental eye roll. The bottom falls out and rain pours down so hard it stings my face. Too far to turn back now, I'm going to get wet either way.

"Well, that just figures," I mumble to myself, and run the rest of the way, getting completely soaked by the time I get to the car. Slinging all of my bags across the seat, I jump in and clumsily search for something to dry off my hands and face with, thankfully finding several fast-food napkins they always give you too many of in the bags. Cramming the key in the ignition, I turn the radio on and drive out of the parking lot to a complete traffic standstill on Blossom Street. Apparently, the University of South Carolina baseball game has been cancelled due to rain and with everyone leaving at the same time, traffic is backed up all the way from Huger Street to Park Street. Working for the university does have its perks, but there are certainly some disadvantages also, like the traffic congestion during baseball and football games, since both stadiums are located downtown.

I look to the right and see several sets of blue lights and people standing in the rain, one guy with his arms swinging wildly like he is trying to explain how his Lexus seems to be connected at the bumper with the Malibu in front of it, and the other, an officer standing in front of him who has a look of defeat on his face. I know he is probably thinking how much he hates working rainy days. Just great, one more thing to make the day even longer.

So, instead of my usual right turn, I make a left and head out of town to take the long way home. I pass through the traffic lights of the city and travel along Assembly Street to the fairgrounds and football stadium to make the turn on Shop Road. From this point, it is a long, straight two-lane road that leads to I-77. The farther out of town I drive, the harder it begins to rain, and puddles in the road are splashing up on the windshield each time a car passes in the opposite lane. At least on this side of town the traffic is sparse and there are not many intersections to slow me down. With a heavy sigh, the tension of the day slowly recedes.

Unexpectedly, a single glaring bolt of lightning cuts a jagged path through my line of sight and strikes a tree just a few feet ahead of me, sending sparks and tree bark exploding down onto the roadway. The intense explosion of light temporarily blinds me and thunder bursts so loudly I feel it in my chest making my heart skip a beat. Slamming on brakes, my Corolla slides on the wet asphalt, and I shut my eyes tight while firmly gripping the steering wheel in anticipation of hitting something. Feeling the car stop and rock abruptly, I open my eyes to find I am mere inches from the guardrail of a short bridge with a small green sign affixed to the top of it.

As the bluish outlines of lightning are slowly fading from my vision, I am struck with the odd thought that the afterimage looks remarkably like a woman in a loose, free-flowing dress. The illusion hangs near the ground for several moments longer and then appears to move in slow wisps of lacy mist toward the edge of the road and simply fades away at the tree line. Puzzled, I convince myself that the brightness of the lightning must have burned my eyes. My heart is pounding so hard I can feel its rhythm drumming in my fingertips against the steering wheel, and I let go to flex my fingers and hands several times to get the blood flowing in them again. Rain is pouring in sheets so thick I can barely make out the sign right in front of me and I have to squint to read it: Hidden Creek.

At the same time, I take a deep breath and shake my head to clear the shock, I realize static is drifting softly from the radio. "Lord that was close!" I say as I shift the car into reverse to move away from the edge of the bridge. Pausing for a moment, I see the skid marks in the grass before me, and I am absolutely amazed I did not hit the bridge rail. Considering myself lucky, I put the car in drive and pull onto the roadway to cross the bridge. As soon as my tires pass from the asphalt of the road to the concrete of the overpass, a strange, icy numbness washes over me. More like, flows through me.

It's a fleeting sensation that rapidly wells up and recedes before I can blink my eyes or draw a breath – a feeling more like a rise and fall in consciousness, or the swelling of a wave the split second before it breaks and rushes to shore. All at once, the windows in the car fog up and an overpowering silence consumes within a vacuum, creating an overwhelming sense of emptiness and solitude. The hair rises on the back of my neck from fright as my senses are inundated with the smell of old wet leaves and damp earth, and I am suddenly so cold I can feel the warmth seeping out of my fingertips.

Strange, unfamiliar scenes begin to move and tumble through my mind in a slideshow, similar to an old movie flickering on a dingy white screen or a fluttering sheet hung to dry in the wind. Caught in a strong magnetic-like current pulling toward one side of the bridge, I am subconsciously aware that I am slowly leaning in that direction, but I am so entranced with the mental images I am unable to control my movements. All of my attention sharply focuses on a single picture, that of a young woman dancing gracefully in the night, her dress and hair flowing in slow motion around her, and then all at once, an explosion of fiery red light that abruptly ends the slideshow. And then, just as fast as it started, all of it is gone. My first impression is that it is just the adrenaline from skidding off of the road. But then again, it's almost like *déja vú*

I pull off onto the shoulder of the road just after I cross the bridge and open the windows a bit to breathe some fresh air and collect my faculties enough to drive on. My heart is hammering, I have broken out in a cold sweat, and something dreadful is lurking just beneath the surface of my thoughts. As soon as I leave the bridge, the windows clear of the condensation. Looking in the rearview mirror, I expect to see a bank of thick, white fog behind me but there is nothing there and I am left wondering what has come over me.

After crossing the bridge, I am unable to shake this weird, uneasy feeling for several hours. Arriving at the comfort of home brings little relief to my weariness; I am apprehensive and nervous, and my hands tremble so badly that I am dropping things. An eerie, deafening silence is invading the walls of the house like I have never heard before, a pin-drop stillness, like the hush of the dead greeting me in each room. Tremendous pressure is weighing me down, similar to being bogged down under water with only the echo of my heartbeat pounding against my eardrums and the agony of my lungs aching to fill with air. I drop a few chunks of ice into an empty glass and fill it from the tap. I turn, and the glass slips from my grasp and crashes to the floor in slow motion. I stare blankly at the shattered pieces of glass and water puddle on the kitchen floor and try to piece together the bizarre events of the day. I am confused, and lost within my own thoughts.

During the next two weeks, life moves at a lumbering pace, oddly dragging through time, making minutes feel like hours. Work has been more than busy, so I am not surprised that complete exhaustion has set in by Wednesday afternoon. Leaving work at the usual time, I am forced to take the long way home again—traffic has stopped on Blossom Street because of fans going to the rescheduled baseball game. I don't like what I hear on the radio, so I put *The Eagles' Greatest Hits* CD in the player and turn the volume up loud to sing along. The sun shines brightly and with the window rolled down, the fresh air makes me feel fairly refreshed even though it has been such a stressful week. " . . . to the Hotel California . . . such a lovely place . . .

" I sing along at the light at Blair Road waiting for it to turn green. "And still those voices are calling from far away . . . wake you up in the middle of night just to hear . . . "

The music abruptly stops and roaring static blares

from the speakers as a wave of doom cascades through me. The hopelessness is so overwhelming that I am afraid I will pass out and my hands are shaking so violently that I can barely stay on the road. Easing off of the gas, I steer to the side of the road and stop just short of the rail to Hidden Creek Bridge. I close my eyes and press my icy cold hands to my temples as I try unsuccessfully to block out the ghostly images rapidly flashing through my mind.

Leaning into the steering wheel while listening to the sound of the passing cars, I slip into the trance of a mild daydream. Lazily closing my eyes, I slip deeper into the reverie of watching swirling colors ebb and flow together then slowly blend into a rippling pool of dark crimson fluid motion behind my eyelids. There's that odor of wet leaves again and I sense something is horribly wrong. Subconsciously, I realize with each passing car I can hear a jumble of voicelike sound all around me and I start to slip out of the daze. Tires slosh against the wet asphalt as a large truck passes by and I hear a whispery "Hear me?" Sitting up with a sudden start, panic fills my chest as chill bumps spread out on my arms and neck. Hyperventilating, I think, *Oh, no . . . not again!*

"What the heck is going on?" I ask myself aloud. Now I am hearing things. This is crazy and just can't be real; I know I am stressed out but this is just ridiculous. Weird feelings, hearing things, seeing things . . . I am convinced I am losing my grip on sanity.

"Come to me . . . " softly echoes in the watery swooshes of a small car's tires.

"Listen!" a young woman's voice screams as another fluttering catches my eye and I quickly turn my head to look. Nothing is there but the trees. I scrunch my eyebrows together and try to get this crazy notion out of my head. Nervously, I crank my car and step on the gas pedal. Letting out a deep sigh, I hurry off trying to escape whatever is causing me such anguish. As I am speeding away, I glance in my rearview mirror and for just a split second a feeling of profound sorrow grips my soul and I burst into tears. A dull pain begins to swell in my head, and I start seeing the slivers of light and spots in my peripheral vision that signal an oncoming migraine. I vow to myself to never go near that bridge again.

I am having a hard time concentrating on anything without images of the bridge filling my thoughts. Every time I see a certain color of bright red, chills cover my body and an uneasy sensation floods through me. I am filled with a deep sense of restlessness that makes me afraid to even look over my shoulder for fear something dreadful may be lurking behind me or in the shadows. It's a hollow, cold pit in my stomach a lot like the panic that comes when something brushes against me while swimming in deep murky water. The dark is unsettling and I have a hard time sleeping without the security of a nightlight, and, when I do sleep, I have a recurring dream that haunts me.

The dream is broken into countless fragments – there is music and a woman's long dark hair falling behind her as she dances. She is laughing but I can't see her face. Bursts of red, yellow, white, and blue fill the air; fireworks perhaps? Shadows shifting in the streetlights and blurred movements in crowded rooms. Outside at night on a busy downtown street, with cars and people passing by, she nervously slips into the passenger side of a white sports car. Screams ring out in total darkness. There is the image of an open car trunk strewn with miscellaneous news-papers, magazines, and a duffel bag, and the distinct smell of new leather. The woman walking into the woods from the edge of a bridge rail. She is crying. A tall, thin man who walks in shadows. Piercing silence. Nothing but darkness, and then, intense explosions of brilliant red.

Ruby red.

Two months have passed since the last time I crossed the bridge. I am unable to think clearly anymore, much less concentrate on anything. Every time I see the color red, a chilling rush of adrenaline flows through my veins and the whole world turns on its edge. I get the sensation I am falling facefirst into blackness and I can't stop myself. Paranoia is setting in. Am I being followed? I nervously look behind me at almost every step and I find nothing.

Stress grows, causing headaches and tension to plague me at all hours. Agonizing migraines are becoming more frequent, bringing my daily activities to a standstill. Sleep is almost a thing of the past. Lying awake for hours, my nights are consumed with apprehension and worry. If I sleep, I toss and turn between the same dreams of her and waking; if I am awake, all of my thoughts are haunted by that voice. *Her* voice.

Tonight's attempt at sleep has been no different. The same dream steals my rest. It is fitful and shadowy, and I wake in a cold sweat with the sheets twisted around me. I glance over at the clock.

2:15 a.m.

I am so tired I can barely crawl out of bed and my head is throbbing with pain. Thinking a shower might help relax me, I turn the water on as hot as I can possibly stand it and step in. The water is soothing as it cascades from my neck, across my shoulders, and down my back. I close my eyes and let the tension slowly seep out of my body and pool around the drain with the swirling water . . . swirling . . .

Swirling colors bleed into a watery shade of deep vermillion with the intensity of a sunset after a violent storm flood through my mind. My knees are suddenly so weak I can barely stand, so I turn the water off and towel dry. A heavy mist covers the mirror making it look ghostly white in the diffused light of the steamy bathroom. Just as I glance away, something catches my attention: a large droplet of water sluggishly forms near the bottom of the mirror and begins sliding deliberately along the surface of the glass—but it is going up instead of down! I cautiously take a step toward the glass and lean in to curiously focus on what is happening. Breathless and wide-eyed, as though I am under a spell, I watch the blob slowly divide into two, then four. In one swift burst, hundreds of tiny quivering beads rise from the surface of the foggy glass being drawn out by some powerful, unseen force. Bringing my trembling hands to my mouth to suppress a terrified scream, I watch the small drops skitter and dance along with their reflections as they form the letters of a silent message: **COME TO ME**

The words glare at me as the water begins to run on the frosty mirror; heavy streams bleed from the bottom of the letters leaving clear paths in their wakes like gaping wounds on the surface of the glass. Long trailing streaks flow silently down, forming small pools on the countertop beneath the mirror.

Taking several quick steps backward, I hit the wall and gasp in fright, my heart beating so hard I hear the rush of it in my ears, and as I turn to run out of the bathroom, I begin falling into a tunnel of absolute darkness. My breath billows out in front of me in a cloud of white as I begin shivering because the room's temperature has dropped a full thirty degrees. As darkness envelops me, my ears begin to hum louder, and I smell the odor of deep, wet earth that reminds me of the bottom of an old leaf pile that dad and I would turn over to dig for earthworms for fishing when I was little. My head is pounding so hard it feels as if my skull will split at its seams at any minute.

The last thing I hear before losing consciousness is a soft voice calling out, *Someone is crying.* My thoughts trail off as I lose consciousness.

Opening my eyes to the ceiling fan slowly spinning above me, my sentient thoughts begin seeping back into my brain and I am aware the headache has dissipated. Lying sideways on the bed, I am remarkably calm for what has just happened. Slowly, I sit up. At first I think I have been dreaming again. No . . . I'm still wrapped in a towel and my hair is wet. Standing up, I glance through the door to the bathroom at the faint outlines of letters remaining on the frosty glass. I stare at them for a long moment and think to myself I should be terrified. Surprisingly, I am not. The clock by the bed reads 3:08 a.m. in softly glowing blue numbers that cast an eerie glow in the room.

A mysterious supernatural force is nudging me; I need to go somewhere. I have to find something, I don't know what it is, but I have to find it. I am being drawn to something so powerfully that I cannot resist; gravity is strong and my limbs feel heavy and sluggish. Numb and in a daze, I clumsily hurry to get dressed. Pulling on an old T-shirt and pair of jeans, I slip into my boots and grab my keys and cell phone. Without knowing exactly why, I walk out the back door, lock it, and get in the car. Navigating the roads, I realize that I am being led involuntarily to some unknown destination, like someone else is in control and I am just along for the ride. There is very little traffic to slow me, so I know instinctively where I am going as soon as I steer toward the onramp to Highway 77 and see the familiar curves of the road ahead of me in my headlights. A growing storm in the distance declares its presence with heat lightning flickering brilliantly within the clouds, making them glow briefly with a beautiful pink-orange hue. Even this early in the predawn hours, the temperature is nearly unbearable mixed with humidity so high it is like a damp blanket on the skin. In spite of the heat, my hands are as cold as ice.

I recognize the road sign ahead that points the way to the exit ramp at Shop Road. I do not even take the time to hit the brakes or put on my turn signal as I spin the wheel in that direction.

As I speed toward Hidden Creek Bridge, I should be afraid, but I'm not. I should stop, but I can't. I shouldn't go, but I am. I pull over and stop my car in the thick grass on the roadside about ten feet from the rail on the bridge. With dire uncertainty, I step out of the car and onto the thick grass. The sign that reads Hidden Creek glows eerily green in the beam of my headlights as I stand silently and stare into the dark shadows beneath the trees. Something unearthly has brought me here. I don't know what it is, but I have to find out why I have been drawn to this bridge by this unnatural force.

I pop open the trunk and fumble through my roadside assistance bag for the emergency flashlight, hoping the batteries aren't dead. Flipping the switch several times on and off, and satisfied the light will work, I close the trunk and walk slowly toward the bridge rail. As I carefully begin making my way down the steep embankment to the creek bed below, tightness rises in my chest and fear grips tightly at my throat and I have to stop. After a few seconds, I mutter to myself, "No. I can't stop now . . . ", and continue on into the night.

Shining the flashlight around in random directions, I see nothing but faint outlines of trees and rocks, and an occasional reflection of light darting off of the water onto the low-hanging branches above the creek. The wind picks up; the storm must be getting closer because the mugginess in the air presses down heavily on me causing sweat to drip from my forehead and my shirt to stick uncomfortably to my back. Lightning flashes brightly, blinding me momentarily in the night's shadows.

Deeper and deeper into the darkness I try to carefully make my way down the steep bank and end up sliding most of the way after losing my footing. Reaching the bottom, I brush off my hands and jeans, and shine the beam of my light around in search for anything that can reveal to me why I am here.

"Nothing . . . " I mutter to myself and stop. Standing in the middle of the woods, at almost dawn, I wonder to myself if I have finally slipped the bounds of reality and into madness.

The creek bed is wide and muddy, in spite of the creek itself being only a few feet across and very shallow. The banks gently slope upward about ten feet and are covered in moss and dead leaves. The remaining twenty or so feet are steeply hollowed out from erosion, and the banks are covered in tangles of tree roots and patches of green lichen, moss and wild fern.

"Shh," I hear the breeze whisper through the branches above me. Strange echoes surround me as my mind spins out of control into an abyss of panic. There has to be an explanation why I am here. What in the world has brought me here?

Looking up and all around at my surroundings, I gather my bearings and begin to make my way farther into the chasm the creek flows through. Having gone only about twenty feet, I stop again, bewildered by my unfamiliar surroundings. Standing here in the dark, with only a single beam of light to see by, I suddenly realize the smell is overwhelmingly familiar: damp leaves mixed with dirt. I draw in a sharp gulp of air in fright and exhale thick white fog. The air around me drops rapidly to about thirty degrees and the sweat on my skin turns to a glistening layer of frost. To no avail, I try to warm myself by blowing into my hands several times.

This is crazy, I think to myself as I look above me at the towering oaks and pines with their spindly, crooked branches stretched out eerily like distorted arms covering the creek bed, hiding it from the world. The night noises and the coming storm bring the sound of a thousand whispering voices all around me, blending together in a pulsing cacophony of echoes.

"Hear . . . " the leaves rustle in the branches above. "Am . . . " as I shift my feet in the decaying leaves below.

There is an overpowering sensation that I am crossing a dimensional plane, like I am drifting in to a different time and place. Turning slowly, I barely have a chance to move my feet when I strike something with my left toe. I aim the flashlight down at my feet expecting a rock or branch; instead, something slithers quickly out of the light making me gasp out loud. Panicking, I shine the beam all around my feet as I take several steps backward to get away from whatever it is. The light finally hits it and it darts away again. Relieved, I realize it is just a large grey and brown speckled salamander. Wiping the cold sweat from my forehead and eyes as I catch my breath, I point the light toward it one more time. As the slimy creature wiggles under the dark mud, it dislodges a piece of something black with a hint of metal that has a strangely familiar shape to it. I lean over and grasp the object and gently coax it from its hold in the thick muck. A knife, about seven inches in length, releases with a slight sucking sound as the blade loses its grip from the mud.

Curiously turning the muddy knife in my shivering hand, I can see that great care went into its making. The blade is finely shaped with a gentle upward slope of the cutting edge and tooling marks along the spine at the thumb rise. The metal is discolored and pitted with age and element exposure, but not rusted or corroded like ordinary carbon steel would be. The black handle appears to be some sort of plastic—Micarta maybe, since it is still in good condition in spite of being immersed in mud. The handle is curved inward in several places so when it is held in the hand, it fits the fingers and palm like a glove. Looking closely, I can barely make out something written on the blade; I slide my thumb against the metal near the finger guard to wipe away a clump of the sticky mud. There, beneath the smear, E WHITE is stamped into the blade; on the opposite side, the number 024.

Lightning crackles through the air and thunder

booms deafeningly, raising the hairs on the back of my neck and startling me so bad that I drop the knife back into the mud. In the flash of lightning, the shadows spread out and move around me like phantoms on the prowl.

Paralyzed with fear, I open my mouth to scream, but terror robs me of my voice. With my heart pounding wildly, my stomach knotting in panic and my legs weak and twitching, the brutal cold settles into my bones as goose bumps spread over my body. White misty breath billows out of my mouth and nose in long thick puffs. Swinging the flashlight around wildly in front of me, I am acutely aware that I have lost all sense of my bearings and I can't remember if I crossed the creek or not, or from which direction I came. At the same moment, the first huge drops of rain tap against the leaves above me and I hear the roar of the coming downpour. The rain is icy against the frosty air around me and shocks me back to my senses. Turning to run back to the car, my foot catches on something unseen and throws me forward. Tumbling to the ground on my hands and knees, the flashlight flies from my grasp and goes spinning out of control into the creek in front of me. Stretching to try to catch it, I splash facefirst into the swampy mire and cry out a loud groan.

In the harsh whispers of the rustling tree branches overhead, I hear her voice. "Hear . . . am . . . "

Lightning flashes brightly overhead and the rain

pours down on my aching back as I lie facedown in the thick, slimy mud where little rivulets of water are flowing down the embankment from the tree line to the creek below. Bogging up to my wrists and ankles in the slick muck, I slowly struggle to my feet and look up ahead at the flashlight. Taking a few hesitant steps forward, I lean over to pick up the flashlight and a glint of red in the path of yellow light shining on the mud catches my eye. Not just any color red, but the intense rouge of a fine ruby.

"Hear . . . " The branches scrape together.

"Hear . . . " The leaves rustle. "Am . . . "

Tick, tick, tick — my brain processes the sounds. *Hear, . . . am.* Thunder explodes through the forest at the same moment the meaning hits me. The wind is crying "HERE I AM!"

Gingerly reaching down into the cold, slippery muck, I lift out a mud-covered ring; the gold is warm in my stone-cold hand. Mystified, I stare at it for a moment before I realize that it is more than just a ring, it is an ornate ruby ring soaked and encrusted with dirt and mud. I pull up my wet shirttail and wipe the stone off to get a better look at it. Holding it up with wet and dirty trembling fingers, I look curiously at the elaborately scrolled band set with a single large oval-shaped ruby encircled by a dozen tiny diamonds. The pigeon-blood-colored gemstone is stunningly faceted and reflects the lightning brilliantly, casting tiny red pinpoints of light on my dirty fingers. Shining the flashlight on it and turning it as the rain washes it clean, my eyes focus past it onto a patch of mossy earth barely illuminated by my flashlight beam. Lying on its side, smiling eerily from the edge of the tree line, a moldy, mud-stained human skull that is discolored by time, stares vacantly at me. A thin stream of rainwater trickles out from the bottommost eye socket like a little river of tears. All at once, the cold begins drawing out of me, from my feet up and out through my shoulders, and warmth seeps back into my bones as I hear the earth around me let out a heavy sigh of relief. The rain tapers to a stop and the first rays of the morning sun begin to break through the clouds and make their way through the canopy of dripping leaves.

One week later, in the *State* newspaper, the following article is published:

SUSPECT CONFESSES TO MURDER DAYS AFTER REMAINS IDENTIFIED

Columbia: Coroner Glenn Dougal says the remains found on Friday have been positively identified as those of Amanda Kingston. Her death has been ruled a homicide.

Kingston went missing in 2000
after leaving a New Year's Eve
party. She was 21 years old.
A suspect was identified through
maker's marks and the serial
number engraved on a custom-
made knife found at the scene.
Sheriff Jon Brady said suspect
Johnathan Taylor issued a full
confession on Monday when he
was brought in for questioning in
reference to the knife purchase
and the disappearance of
Kingston. Records kept by the
custom knife maker indicate the
knife had been purchased by
Taylor in October, 1999, just
three months prior to Kingston's
disappearance.

She was buried quietly on a warm, sunny afternoon in a small family church cemetery on the outskirts of town. The graveyard was modest and tidy, with each wind-worn headstone laid out to face east so they could bear the names of the departed to the rising sun each morning. The ceremony was humble, with few grievers other than her family who silently departed after paying their respects. As her devoted mother lingered mournfully by the grave with her hand tenderly resting upon Amanda's pale silver casket, a gentle breeze blew across the graveyard and softly whispered through the surrounding pines.

The ruby ring, a family heirloom that had been passed down several generations on her mother's side of the family, was a sixteenth birthday gift from Amanda's grandmother. Shortly after Amanda's remains were recovered, it was returned to her mother, who now wears it on an unassuming gold chain around her neck as a constant reminder of undying love.

Once in a while, someone slips into the quiet cemetery under the cover of night and places a single ruby red rosebud on her headstone, a symbol that the spirit is stronger than the life it possesses.

Far across town, in an old, shallow creek bed below a bridge, radiant beams of the afternoon sun creep through the shadows to the peaceful ground below, and a bird softly chirps a simple, cheerful song.

IS IT ME?

BY NATHAN R. RIZER

EVEN AS A KID, I felt something ominous about the big white house on a two-lane highway in the middle of nowhere, South Carolina. I spent a week there most summers with my favorite aunt and uncle.

The house possessed an uncomfortable quiet during the day, and at night, an uneasiness that seemed anything but quiet. Thirty-five years ago, at least, and I can still see every inch of the house clearly — inside and out.

My aunt was always in the kitchen, and I was given free reign of the house. I usually spent my days on the screened-in back porch, or, if I were lucky enough to have another kid there, outside. I didn't like to venture to the yard alone.

Just to the right of center in the front yard was a huge tree, oak maybe, but definitely the focal point of the yard. Long, overhanging branches with no foliage and low-hanging Spanish moss. That tree drew me to it like a magnet, but when I neared it, the poles reversed and I was repelled so violently that I'd dash to the porch and rush back into the house.

I never wanted to go to sleep in that house. I prayed my mom or dad would come get me and save me from another night of staring at the closet door, or maybe if I just pretended I was asleep on the couch, I could stay put and wouldn't have to go in that bedroom. Was I scared? Yes and no. But of what? The closest thing I had seen to a horror movie was *Close Encounters*, and I've never lived near enough to a trailer park to worry about being probed by space invaders. Why, at seven years old, did I feel so afraid? Not just of the dark, but of something else — something *in* the dark. The summer visits stopped when my relatives sold the house and moved to Florida.

Some thirty years later, I visited with that aunt and uncle when they came to South Carolina for a reunion. Every hair on my neck stood straight. As casual as could be, my aunt began talking about the old house. She spoke of the voices of children she could hear playing around the big tree in the front yard. She heard them but never saw them. My uncle told of other sounds and voices they heard in the house. That house was my first memory of something that truly scared me. It seemed there was good reason.

I've heard and read much of ghostly occurrences. Do I think a deceased principal roams the halls of Brookland Cayce High School — slamming locker doors and scaring kids into behaving to avoid detention so they won't be in those corridors alone after school? Probably not. And I've taken my turn down Old State Road in Cayce, where stopping a car supposedly results in a stalled vehicle and the appearance of a ghost. We stopped the car on the bridge and got out. Imagine our disappointment when we saw nothing, the car started, and we simply drove off.

The noises heard in the old cemetery near Trinity Episcopal Church in downtown Columbia are more likely than not one of our city's homeless rather than a Confederate era veteran, but Google "Haunts in Columbia" and all of this will be found. Surely there are more. An area with so much rich history — there has to be more. Not the legends everyone writes about, but stories from normal houses in average neighborhoods that only the residents know about and never speak of.

For instance, the apartment I used to have in the midtown section. Hardwood floors and a view of the skyline within walking distance of every convenience and with rent that was about a third of what it should have been. Seemed like a steal. That is, until the night I decided to sleep with the bedroom door open.

SLAM woke me the first night. What the hell was it? The lights of the city that usually lit up my apartment weren't doing so. My place was at ground level. Had someone broken in? My bedroom door was shut, and I'd made it a point to leave it open that night. Nobody was in my apartment, but the bedroom door had clearly been closed as I slept. I wrote it off to—well, to whatever we write those things off to. You know, those unlikely explanations we use so that we feel better about a bump in the night.

The next night I left my bedroom door open and placed a clothes basket in front of it so it wouldn't be moved by a draft. Again the door shut—this time with enough force to move the basket. The following night I placed the basket in front of the door, only this time filling it up with books. No way was the door going to close on its own. It didn't. That night I awoke to a crash and the bedside lamp falling on my head. The battle of wills was won. I slept with the door closed for the remaining few days and nights I stayed there though sleep ceased to be restful even when the door was tightly shut.

At that time, the girlfriend I lived with was a flight attendant and was seldom home. I was a bartender and did a lot of my sleeping during the day— probably a good thing since nights had grown increasingly unnerving. My last memory in that apartment was waking up from a nap, sick to my stomach. I felt pretty out of it but awake enough to be happy that my girlfriend had come home unexpectedly and crawled in beside me in bed. I could feel the movement of the bed and the tussle of the blanket being tugged away from me. I smiled and put my arms around her.

I opened my eyes in frozen terror. She wasn't there—nobody was. That was my last day in that apartment. The building was over a hundred years old and had been renovated into apartments. Later, I learned that the landlord couldn't keep our apartment rented and that a girl had been murdered in the shower. I wish I could say that this story was based loosely on an account I'd heard, but the truth is that it happened to me just as I'm describing.

Everybody has childhood memories of the house that nobody lived in, or the old church, or the woods behind a best friend's house. The urban legends are fun to think about when hanging out with friends, but what happens when it stops being fun? What happens when the fear graduates from being entertaining when you're a kid into keeping an adult man up at night? There were the shadows in one house. In another place, I heard footsteps at all hours and there was a door that was always shut, but it gave me chill bumps to walk past that door.

Most recently, my sixth-grade son and I lived in a new complex where there had only been one occupant before us. Why did my son refuse to sleep in his room and want to sleep on the couch every night? He had never done that in any previous residence. This place was the only one where I was one hundred percent positive there was physical contact between something paranormal and myself.

Once a week, I would wake up being tapped on my head or my hand—a distinct three taps each time. I won't forget those taps. I won't ever forget the three scratches I received there either. I wasn't in bed when it happened. The back of my calf began to burn horrifically as I showered one night, and three bright red marks were visible when I toweled off.

Same place, another time—a dark figure stood by my bed, no face, just a black mist of a figure wearing a strange, crooked hat. Maybe human, maybe not, but I remember the sight just as if it were standing in front of me as I write this. There was checking on my son when I heard him call, "Daaadd," only to find him sound asleep. Then there was waking up to 'DAAAADDD!" when my child came screaming into my room, terrified of something he has yet to talk about.

Coincidentally, I found out the only previous resident of my apartment was an acquaintance of mine. I learned this when I received some of her mail that had not been forwarded. One night, when things had been really bad for several days, I Facebooked her, not really expecting a response. She replied immediately and said, "You're scaring the hell out of me right now." She went on to say that her son, close to mine in age, refused to sleep in that same room. She also told me that sometimes when she pulled into her parking place, she'd look up at the window of that apartment and see that her television was on. Once upstairs, she'd find everything was off. Then she began to tell me she could feel someone around her bed at night, and. . .

Her message abruptly ended. I've tried and tried to contact her, but I've never heard from her since then.

Do we open ourselves up to experience these things when we believe or is it possible there has been a presence in most of the places where I've lived? Or is it me?

Today, my son and I moved into a house with an elaborate security system. No one has lived here before, and the land was cleared to build this house. Tonight I lie in my new bed in my new home. My son is spending the night with his grandparents. The footsteps sound closer and closer, but the alarm hasn't activated. My closed bedroom door is opening. I repeat: Is it possible there has been a presence in most of the places I've lived?

Or is it m . . . .

THE DOOR BETWEEN MARY

BY J. MICHAEL SHELL

This story was previously published in 2013 in Pages of Stories *in Canada.*

THE ANCIENT ROMANS named the hottest days of summer after the star Sirius, which rose in their August-morning skies. They called that celestial body "The Dog," and those simmering weeks of heat became known as "The Dog's Days."

Though there may be hotter places on Earth, the low country of South Carolina rivals them all with its stifling air, when those days of the Dog arrive. Even the kudzu weeps in that gruesome scald, while leaves of wild cherry and sweet gum curl like dead men's tongues. Only the Spanish moss seems unaffected, as it lazily hangs in the summer steam—mimicking, with its drooping posture, the misery of every creature there.

But in all that tropical haunt of swelter, there is one place that seems always hotter, always more of a burden to lungs and sinew. It is the site of the ruins of St. Mary's church, pockmarked all around by the sunken graves of her colonial congregation. On the coldest winter day, with frost bejeweling those remnant arches and pane-less windows, one might call those ruins appealing to the eye. But during that time when the Dog reigns over his days, there is no more oppressive place to be, and it's said that even those long dead parishioners seek to escape the wretched burden of their interment there.

Though stories abound concerning malevolent summertime apparitions appearing at this place, their origins are so lost in time that they are nowadays taken lightly—considered to be superstitious ramblings left over from a long gone culture and era. Other than very small children (who shouldn't be told such stories at all) most people who hear these yarns simply laugh. Perhaps it is the distance in time from which the stories have traveled that makes them seem too far removed from modernity to be taken seriously. But there is one such occurrence (which few know about) that took place on the back porch of today—forty years ago, in 1969.

Her name (by coincidence, some would say) was Mary, and her beau was a lad called Will. Mary and Will were just completing their second decade of life in the world, and were little more than full-grown children. But they were hardy children, born and raised in the sultry climes of Northern Georgia, and able to stand the long waves of hot days that were common to that region.

Will and Mary had adopted the ways of many of the youth of their time—wearing their clothing patched, with beads about their necks and flowers braided into their long, wild hair. Like Indians intent to tread lightly on the earth, they clad their feet in soft moccasins. So bedecked, Will and Mary had set out from their tiny Georgia town to make their way far into the North—there to join with others of their ilk who were gathering for a festival of music and camaraderie.

Having no means of transportation of their own, Will and Mary decided to employ the time-honored American tradition of hitching a ride. Though, these days, that practice itself is the source of many a gruesome tale, Will and Mary were fearless in their youth, and most people willing to offer a ride back then were harmless.

As these two young travelers crossed the line into South Carolina, in the back of a farmer's pickup, Mary told Will of her desire to stop in the low country and see the ruins of her namesake saint's church.

"Mamma and Daddy took me there once when I was five years old," she told him. "It was Christmas, and we'd gone to Aunt Emily's in Beaufort for the holidays. I'd never seen anyplace so old and so lovely. I've thought about it all my life, and I want to go back there to see if my memories are true."

"Is it far from the highway?" Will asked, anxious to reach the festival.

"Let's ask the farmer when he lets us out. He said he was only going as far as Beaufort."

When the farmer reached his exit, he pulled over on the ramp to let the strangely clad young people climb out of his truck. "This here's it," he called back to them. "Far north as I'm goin'."

"Could you tell us where to find the ruins of St. Mary's church?" Mary asked him.

"Y'all wantin' to go there?" he asked her, his eyes squinted and his brow furrowed.

"I'd like to see it again," Mary told him. "I haven't been there since I was a little girl."

"Well," the farmer said, rubbing his sunburned neck, "you ain't much more'n a little girl *now,* but if that's where you're wantin' to go, hop back in—I'm passin' right by there."

"That's wonderful!" Mary proclaimed. "Thank you, so much!"

The farmer shook his head as Will and Mary climbed back into his truck.

When the pickup stopped again, on a tiny little road that snaked through a tunnel of overhanging trees, the farmer called out once more to Mary. "It's a hundred yards through them trees to the ruins," he said. "But it's about the hottest place there is this time of year. Only-est thing 'tween folks that lives around here and hell is a screen door!"

"And we just follow this road back to the highway, right?" Will asked.

"Yup. Pro'bly have to hoof it, though. Not many uses this road no more."

"Thanks again!" Mary called, as the farmer drove off.

"You're surely welcome," he said to himself.

Mary smiled at Will's dour face as they made their way through the vines and bramble to find the church. "I thought you were adventurous," she said, teasingly.

"It's just that I've never been up north," Will answered defensively. "I want to get somewhere I've never been."

"Have you ever been *here*?" Mary asked him.

"I've been to South Carolina," he said, despite knowing exactly what she'd meant.

"Look!" Mary said, parting a thick curtain of wisteria vines. "There it is! Isn't it beautiful?"

"Maybe it would be if this was December," Will told her. "But that farmer was right. I can barely breathe."

"Let's get out of this bramble, and it won't be so bad. See how open it is all around the church. And that grass looks like somebody mows it."

"Probably goats gnaw it down," Will said, though no goats, or any other creatures for that matter, were evident. Even insects seemed strangely absent.

"C'mon!" Mary said, starting to run as she came out into the open. "I'll bet it's cooler by those old stone walls."

American Indians, whom Will and Mary somewhat resembled — in costume if not facial feature — often imbibed ritual substances in holy pipes called *chanunpas*. Though Will and Mary's tiny pipe in no way resembled a *chanunpa*, its function was pretty much the same. Sitting on the only-slightly-cooler stones of the church, they sipped smoke from that little pipe. Before long they seemed, like the Spanish moss and the leaves in the trees, to droop and wilt. "I guess it is pretty here, in a hot-as-hell sort of way," Will said, inspired to see beauty by the ritual smoke.

"I'm sleeping here tonight," Mary said, her eyes hooded by lazy eyelids.

"What'll we eat?" Will asked her, his hunger also inspired.

"I've got trail-mix in my pack, and Pemmican jerky. And my canteen's full of water."

"Mine's full, too," he told her. "But I filled it with apple wine."

Mary laughed. "And I've got a candle, so we have all the makin's of a candlelight picnic."

Though the sun went down, the heat never abated. Between ritual smoke and apple wine on practically empty stomachs, Will and Mary lay sleepy in one another's arms as silence and darkness wrapped them. Before long Mary could hear the rhythmic breathing that told her Will was asleep. The darkness around her was complete, but before long she could make out the faint sound of something scraping against earth. "Will," she whispered, touching his arm. "Will, are you awake?"

Will was not awake. At first, a twinge of fear caused Mary to think of waking him. But that twinge left as quickly as it had washed over her. Leaving Will alone, she reached into her pack and found her candle.

There were stars above the clearing in which the ruins stood, but their luminosity did not reach the ground. Outside the circlet of light Mary's candle cast, there was only hot darkness and that faint sound of scraping. Mary followed the strange noise, till it grew louder and more distinct. Then suddenly, as if it had jumped out ahead of her, her candlelight illuminated a small boy who was sitting on the ground and digging with a little tin shovel. Though Mary was startled by the boy's abrupt appearance, she was not afraid. Never had she seen such a beautiful child. His hair was long and all of golden curls. He wore what looked like a tiny, raw-silk shirt and shorts held up by little indigo suspenders. "What are you doing out here?" Mary asked. At first the boy didn't answer her, or even look up, but continued his digging as if intent to find some treasure there in the ground. "Do you live around here?" Mary tried again. "Are you lost?"

When she said that the little boy smiled. It was a beautiful smile, but seemed out of place on such a young child—as if it belonged, somehow, to a wise (or sly) old man. "I'm not lost," the boy said, still without looking up—still intent on his digging. "Perhaps it is *you* who are lost."

"What's your name?" Mary asked him.

"Elijah."

Mary knelt down beside Elijah and peered into the hole he was digging. "Are you looking for something?"

"Of course," he answered in his sweetly lisping, hypnotically pretty voice. "You're going to need a key. Ah—here it is now!"

Elijah reached into the hole he'd been digging and pulled out what looked like a small bone. It could have been a rabbit's leg bone, or perhaps the finger of a full grown human. Holding it out in his palm, Elijah turned his lovely face toward Mary and smiled beatifically as tears streamed from his eyes. "Why are you crying?" Mary asked, suddenly overwhelmed with sadness at seeing the precious child's tears.

"Because I haven't a soul to play with," Elijah told her. "You'll stay and play with me, won't you?" he asked, still smiling and crying at the same time.

Mary felt as if she were once again filled with ritual smoke. Elijah suddenly looked even more beautiful, and the heat seemed to caress her skin and make her want more of it. "Yes," she heard herself whisper.

Elijah rose, took Mary's hand, and walked with her into the darkness. "Where are we going?" Mary asked, her voice sounding as though she were speaking through cotton.

"Home," Elijah told her. "But we must get you properly dressed first. You said you'd play with me, did you not?"

"Yes, but why must I change first?" Mary asked.

"Because you're much too big."

When those two, hand in hand, came to the ruined walls of the church, Elijah gave Mary the little bone he'd uncovered while digging. Then he pointed to a small hole in the wall. "Put your key in there," he said.

As soon as Mary slid the bone into the hole, the sun threw brilliant rays into a clear winter sky. She felt chill air on her suntanned arms. Though this sudden change from dark to day and from heat to cold should have startled her, it did not. What did cause her eyes to widen was the sight of her parents, young and smiling, standing across the clearing. Between them, holding their hands, was a little girl Mary recognized immediately. "It's me!" she said. "It's Christmas day and I'm five years old."

"Yes," Elijah said, just as little Mary freed herself from her parent's fingers and ran across the clearing to the frost-sparkled ruins.

"Look," Mary said to Elijah. "Mamma and Daddy are kissing."

"Yes," he answered. "And you are wandered off behind the church, out of their sight. Come now, let's get you changed."

Elijah took Mary by the hand once more, and pulled her around to the back of the church to find her little self. When the child she'd been saw them coming, she said to Mary, "Hello. Is this your little boy?"

Elijah laughed when the child said that, and the sound of it caused Mary to wince. Then he said, "This is my little girl. Don't you recognize her?"

"You do look very familiar," the girl-child said to Mary.

"She is! Come to her," Elijah said, as Mary dropped to her knees and held out her arms to her five-year-old self.

Little Mary ran into her own arms, then realized it was actually Elijah holding her. "How did you get so big?" she asked him. Then she looked down and saw that she was a child.

"Come!" Elijah said, taking her firmly by the hand. "It's time to go home. Once we're there, we can play forever."

"What about Mamma and Daddy? They'll miss me."

"For a while," Elijah said.

"What about Will?" Mary asked.

"*He'll* never miss you at all."

Unsure of why he'd slept in that ancient churchyard, Will made his way back to the highway and headed north once again. As he held out his thumb to the oncoming traffic, he smiled. "Maybe I'll meet a pretty girl at Woodstock," he thought.

SWAMP MAN

BY ROBERT D. SIMKINS

"GET YOUR HAND outta that water, boy! The gators will pull you in and we'll have to leave you for Swamp Man to finish you off." Grandpa laughed heartily.

I snatched my hand from the swirling, cool, black water as a snake slithered past. My best friend Harry and I were in Gramps' old, beat-up, rusty green bass boat.

For many years, Grandpa Jay had told us stories of the swamp—his favorite fishing hole where the infamous Big Bertha catfish lived and the legend of Swamp Man. Now Harry and I were both ten years old, and for the first time, Grandpa was taking us with him into the swamp.

"Please tell us about Swamp Man," Harry pleaded.

"I don't want to talk about it." Gramps' eyes glazed over. He seemed transported back in time to his personal nightmare of the menacing creature that lurked deep within the swamp—a beast that would rip apart anything that ventured too deeply into the swamp.

The dark, overcast day enveloped us as we boated deeper into the swamp. I imagined that the foul smells were rotting flesh from the many kills Swamp Man had made. Overhanging tree branches cast long, entangling shadows on us like a huge spider web waiting to capture us in its clutches. Grandpa zipped the boat around fallen trees and stumps with ease.

In preparation for this trip with Grandpa and Harry, I'd packed my Swiss Army knife for protection and a knapsack full of Momma's peanut butter and jam sandwiches for my always hungry belly. I pulled out a sandwich and started munching it. The toasted bread oozed grape jam that overflowed and dripped from the corners of my mouth. As I chewed, I thought about what Momma always told me.

"There are special powers in these sandwiches," she would say. "They'll make you grow up big and strong."

Harry looked hungrily at me with puppy dog eyes, so I dug into the sack and gave him a sandwich.

Grandpa pointed into the sky at circling buzzards just ahead.

"There's a dead animal close by," he said.

We passed a half-eaten deer carcass rotting near the bank as the birds dove down into its innards, pecking at it with blood-covered beaks.

"I bet Swamp Man did it." Harry whispered.

We slowed down as we rounded the bend and arrived at Gramps' fishing hole. Grandpa Jay brought the boat to a full stop and dropped the anchor.

"We're here," he mumbled. "Be quiet now, boys. This is where Big Bertha got away from me three years ago."

Harry and I gulped down our sandwiches and baited our hooks with squirming blood worms. As soon as their lines plopped in the water, Gramps and Harry each reeled in a fish nearly as big and fat as my sandwich sack while my line drifted untouched. As the hour got late, the fish stopped biting, and the quiet stillness surrounding us must have reminded Gramps of Swamp Man. He began talking in a hushed tone.

"Daddy and I went deer hunting deep into this here swamp. We walked for hours through the thick, muddy trails before we saw any deer at all, but then Daddy managed to get a seven-point buck with just one shot. On the way home, the swamp got really dark and creepy, and right then, we saw it!" He paused.

Harry and I squirmed in the silence until Grandpa Jay continued. "We heard a loud, awful bellowing noise in front of us about a hundred yards away, and

Daddy motioned for me to get down and be quiet. We crouched behind a prickly thorn bush near the creek bank and watched. I felt my heart pounding like it could jump out of my chest at any minute. The hulking swamp creature stood over seven feet tall, half-man and half-ape. It was covered with thick, matted, brown hair and caked in smelly swamp mud. Its evil sunken eyes were as red as hot blazing coals. It looked like the devil himself.

"Daddy pulled me close to him in a tight hug as we watched the creature rip at Daddy's seven-point buck carcass violently with its hands and teeth, gorging itself with the meat. Its face dripped crimson blood as its hands pulled at the leg bone and tossed it to the ground. The deer's skin tore like it was made of paper. I will never forget what I saw that day."

"You're fibbing, ain't you, Grandpa Jay? There ain't really no Swamp Man, is there?" Harry asked.

Gramps looked at us vacantly. "Oh, he's out there, but don't you boys worry." Grandpa pulled a pearl-handled Colt forty-five pistol from his tackle box. "I got something for him."

The shadows grew longer and deeper as the late-day sun fell behind the trees. Grandpa and Harry had caught about twenty fish between them, but Big Bertha remained safe in the water. I clutched my Swiss Army knife and scoured the banks as we headed back, hoping to get a glance of Swamp Man. It was nearly dusk when Grandpa told me to turn on the big lantern and hold it in the front of the boat so he could see. The light illuminated a large black figure on the far bank moving with us. The tall grasses parted forcefully as the shadow moved in its wake.

"My God, I see it!" Grandpa shouted.

He grabbed the Colt pistol and cocked it. The black mass screamed—a loud, piercing sound that flooded the swamp. Grandpa Jay fired the pistol several times at the shadowy figure. The boat hit a half-submerged log in the creek and began taking on water.

"Help! Grandpa, we're sinking!" I shouted.

Grandpa Jay quickly gunned the motor toward the bank before the boat filled up completely with water.

The shadow was gone.

"The boat's done for. We'll have to camp here for the night and hike home in the morning. Y'all gather up some dry branches so we can get a big fire started." Gramps motioned toward the trees. "Fire will keep that evil devil away," Gramps assured Harry and me.

As the fire blazed strong and tall, I felt warm and safe beside it, but Harry was scared out of his wits and made sure he stayed close to Grandpa.

We all fell asleep to the rhythmic sounds of crickets, toads, and bats flapping all around us as the flames grew dimmer and dimmer. I was awakened late in the night when the swamp became suddenly silent.

Harry and Grandpa Jay were snoring like a hand saw ripping back and forth into a bald cypress tree. I opened my eyes slightly while peering through the fire's swirling, white, smoke. I saw Swamp Man at the edge of camp and reached for my knife. My body trembled and my heart thudded. Suddenly, I was unable to move or speak, I sat paralyzed. The creature moved closer toward me.

Sitting with my back against the tree, I pretended to be asleep as Swamp Man sniffed around the campsite. He snatched up my bag of sandwiches, pressed his nose into the sack, and snorted. I froze, trying to breathe silently so he wouldn't notice me as he took a sandwich out and gobbled it up, smacking loudly. One after another, he gulped down sandwiches. Swamp Man turned toward me, his red eyes staring. I expected him to grab me, but he kept eating—long tongue flicking around his rubbery looking lips and then sucking the grape jam from his fingers. His stench was overwhelming. Grandpa Jay awoke and slapped his hand over his nose.

"What's that awful smell?"

Gramps looked at me then followed my gaze to Swamp Man. Grandpa did not panic but slowly eased his gun toward the monster. The creature, sensing the movement, charged swiftly at him, and then stopped short and shrieked; scaring Grandpa Jay so bad that he dropped the gun.

Swamp Man snatched up the bag of peanut butter and jam sandwiches, snorted at Grandpa, and sped off into the swamp. Grandpa Jay quickly regained his composure, grabbed the gun, and fired a shot into the swamp. The commotion awakened Harry, who burst into tears and cried even longer and louder than before. We sat there for a while trying to recover. In my mind, all I could think about was, "Thank God I had Momma's peanut butter and jam sandwiches."

Grandpa Jay knew that nobody would believe us, just like when he was a kid and everybody thought he was crazy, so we made a pact to keep this night as our secret just like the fishing hole. I still wonder every time I drive past Black Creek Swamp if the creature is still in there. Even after all these years, I never go back to the old fishing hole without bringing a bag full of Momma's peanut butter and jam sandwiches . . . just in case.

YOU SHALL NEVER HAVE OUR HOME

BY TWO RAVENS

OLD NAN STOOD at the stove, her wide strong back to us as she skillfully created the best food anyone could ever hope to eat in an entire life. While her hands moved deftly from pot to oven to sideboard as she saw to this or that dish, her tongue wagged away as it often did. She loved sharing those tales from Africa that had been passed down to her by her mamma as much as we loved to hear them. My husband, Dalton, had been raised on Old Nan's stories along with her cooking and he was quite addicted to both. I can't say that I blame him, though.

When I arrived at this plantation as a young bride some twenty years ago, I was greeted by Old Nan on the evening of my wedding. She'd come bringing a hot cup of ginger tea and an old folktale about an African queen that had me enthralled. At once, I loved her stories as much as did Dalton.

As she cooked for us one night, twenty years later, near the end of the War Between the States, we sat on simple wooden chairs right there in the kitchen listening to one of her fantastical tales.

Some ladies, and gentlemen as well, would've considered it quite improper to sit in the kitchen and listen to a house slave telling tales, but Dalton and I never paid folk like that any mind, and we never will. They might be proper, but they are missing out on some very good stories, that's for sure. That night she told a chilling tale of dark creatures that came hunting you in the night to eat your soul right out of your chest.

"Dey be leavin' you empty like a shell, but you be still livin'. You be livin' empty fo dem creatures done eat yo soul all up," she told us.

I couldn't help but shudder. Though Nan had not turned to see my distress, she felt it. Nan was aware of many things without having to see them.

"Now, you doan be letting that scare you, Miss Lorelei," she told me, tone half comforting and half reprimanding. "You and Mr. Dalton got souls too tough fo any creature to eat."

And we all laughed. That night was the last one to be full of laughter and delicious food for a long time to come.

I've never been able to abide the color blue since

the Yankees invaded and ravaged our beloved home. It was as if Nan had somehow felt them coming the night before — as if her dark tale of the soul-eating creatures had been some sort of warning.

I have always thought of our plantation, the Bell Flower, as a woman, and those blue devils treated her with shocking and rough disrespect, devoid of any semblance of regard what-so-ever.

Her lush fields, thick with rice, were burned. I remember screaming with pain and rage as I watched the wicked flames eat the heart of our precious land. Never in my life had I ever imagined I could feel so helpless. Of course with times being what they were, I imagined what it might be like if the Yankees did show up to take what they felt was their due from us.

It was war time, after all, and we'd gotten letters from cousins in Virginia relating enough tales of atrocities committed by Yankees to give me nightmares. Still, I somehow felt that we'd manage to hold on better than others in the face of the devils in blue. I believed my strong, brave husband could drive them out and that they would eventually quell before his firm iron will or at least his persuasive tongue. He is very good with words. Why, I've always said he'd do just fine if he ever took up politics, but he'll have none of it.

Dalton wasn't able to stop the Yankees from taking all they wanted from our home and destroying all they didn't want. The Yankee devils were very wasteful monsters. If they didn't want something, they wouldn't leave it for the rightful owners, because they would like us all to die a harsh death from starvation or worse.

After they set fire to all our fields, they worked their way to our house. The once welcoming, homey walls of the manor house that had always radiated an enveloping feeling of well-being was turned into a cold, uninviting shell by the Yankees in a matter of hours.

"You may strip our home down to her bones, but she shall never be yours," I told them — back straight, voice grim, and face proud.

"You shall never have our home!"

"You just step aside, little lady, before you get hurt," replied one of the devils in blue.

His scruffy black beard proclaimed him to be no gentleman, so I spit in his face.

After screaming until my throat was raw and fighting them with my bare hands like a mad woman until the brutes knocked me down, all I could do was watch in a state of dull misery with a healthy amount of hatred thrown in for good measure.

Dalton's four sleek hunting hounds were sent into a protective frenzy, attacking the legs of the Yankee's blue uniforms when they saw their master and his home threatened. They were promptly run through with bayonets for their pains. Dalton had been a soldier in the Confederate army before having his lower left leg shot off during the very first week of fighting. He'd been sent home before he'd seen much of the war, and I must confess to having been grateful. Old Nan's nephew had carved him a wooden leg and it served him just fine. Though he'd not seen much of the fighting before getting wounded badly enough to be sent home, he still met the Yankees with a sword in his hand. As he was quite outnumbered, he was stripped of it quickly, and his favorite throwing knives as well. My heart could've busted with pride, though. He'd been so brave.

Disarmed, Dalton stood in the doorway to the kitchen, face grim as the Yankee monsters moved around him as though he weren't even there. Their boots clomping on the wooden floor made me feel sick. They were unwanted in our home, yet they would not leave.

When they were at last gone, no one was left on the Bell Flower plantation except for myself, Dalton, and Old Nan. The blue clad devils had freed all our other slaves, practically forced them to leave, though some of the little turncoats were more than glad to do so I am afraid.

When they'd first come barging into the house, one of the evil Yankees had actually laid hands on Old Nan, turning her away from the stove with his hands on her shoulders. He'd told her to put her spoon down and take her freedom. She'd hit him in the face with that red hot spoon and loudly proclaimed that she'd never leave her family and her home. Not for any blue devil monster or for anyone else either.

It was very hard for us after the Yankee invasion of our home. We had no food, no clothes other than what was on our backs, and very few tools or other wherewithal with which to make more. As the Yankee devils had destroyed our property I remember them laughing and telling us that now we would learn how our slaves felt. They were fools, though, who knew nothing about slaves. At least not our slaves, for they had been well cared for. We'd never mistreated them nor left them to do without as the Yankees had done to us.

For once, I was glad that Dalton and I had never been able to have children as this war-ravaged Charleston was no place for innocent babies. No child should have to grow up in such shameful hardship where there was no help to be had. When we ventured out to assess the damage to neighboring properties, those fellow plantation owners we did encounter practically looked through us. Their eyes were full of despair, and they had nothing to say and no help to give. It seemed all of Charleston, South Carolina, had been given no mercy by the North. They'd not broken our pride, though.

Though our plantation was burned and barren, it was still ours. As I'd sworn to those devil Yankees, they hadn't been able to take our home! Eventually things got better, if slowly. Some of Dalton's relatives moved into the house a few years after the war ended, and began to replant the fields. Finally our Bell Flower was lush and grand once again. Seeing her so restored made me cry every day for quite some time, though I can assure you that the tears were of joy and gratitude.

With the plantation restored, and life pleasant once more, the years seemed to fly by. Our relatives had children, and those children grew up proud and strong on the plantation. Then they got families of their own and moved away, leaving the place to the three of us once more. Things meandered along so peacefully until I looked out of the window one day and got quite a start. There was what looked like a gigantic mechanical bird made all of metal in the sky. It was flying directly over the house, but its wings never flapped like a regular bird. A loud, roaring sound filled the air, and I just knew it had to be one of Nan's monsters come to get us.

We'd survived the Yankees, though, and we'd not be letting any monster eat our souls. That thought didn't keep me from screaming out, but by the time Nan and Dalton made it into the room and over to the window to see what had me carrying on so, the monster was much smaller. It was flying very fast, but they were still able to make it out. Thankfully, its roar had also diminished as it winged away across the sky.

"I did never see such in all my days," Nan

proclaimed fervently, making a sign against evil in the direction of the window.

It didn't stop there either. We continued to see as well as to hear strange things. The mechanical birds eventually became so common that we didn't bother to call each other when we saw them anymore. Soon there were other episodes. One day Dalton came running inside from where he'd been inspecting the fields as he was often fond of doing. His eyes were wide and astonished as he told us of seeing an odd carriage sort of machine that, like the flying monster, also seemed made all out of metal. According to him, it had no horses or other animals pulling it along, yet it had sped by nearly as fast as had the flying monster!

"I could swear it had glass windows too," he added breathlessly.

At that Nan snorted.

"Now that be some fine rubbish, Master Dalton, and you know it! Ain't no way to be getting' glass winders in no carriage."

Dalton shook his head in befuddlement, but stuck firmly to his story, glass windows and all.

The next day, it was Nan who called us to the kitchen window to hear the strange nearby sounds of children's laughter accompanied by loud music unlike anything we had ever heard before. It had a thumping beat overlaid by rhythmic talking.

"Now, have you ever heard anything of the like,"

Old Nan demanded.

We silently shook our heads while trying to lean out of the window for a better look, but we may as well not have bothered, for there was no one in sight. No strange flying monsters or horseless carriages with glass windows either. In a few seconds, the sounds of music and children's laughter had faded.

Though these occurrences were strange and unsettling indeed, there was nothing to be done for it. Old Nan became quite shaken and assured Dalton and me more than once that we were being haunted. That or infested by "dem creatures after eatin' our souls." I told her not to fret herself over it as whatever oddity this was that visited us from time to time, unlike the Yankee devils, they had caused us no harm. It only provided something for us to wonder over, and nothing more. Dalton seemed to agree with me, but there was no convincing Nan. She didn't argue with me outright, though, only shaking her dark head and muttering under her breath as she set about banging pots and pans in the kitchen just about as loud as she could.

The final such strange happening occurred the next evening. Nan was cooking and we sat in the kitchen listening to another one of her stories. This time about an old African bone man who could use chicken bones to read the future. Fascinated, I was just opening my mouth to ask Nan if she could try doing the same thing, when I heard a voice speaking so close behind me that it made me jump nearly out of my skin.

"The Bell Flower Plantation is one of the better preserved homes from the Civil War times that Charleston has to offer. As you can see, the restoration was nearly flawless right down to the old wood stove. The Wellington couple, along with their cook, were killed right here in this very kitchen, defending their home from the Yankees."

The voice had taken on a hushed quality, and the last words spoken were accompanied by several gasps. Someone, or what appeared to be several someones, had strolled right into our home and were playing some sort of very rude and tasteless joke. Bringing up that awful time when the Yankee devils had invaded our home was bad enough, but to pretend that we'd been killed? To mock us in this way was unforgivable.

I jumped to my feet and turned quick as a flash to glare the new intruders directly in the face, but no one was there. Before I could think what to do, that voice was speaking again, and I stood frozen, listening to it.

"One of the Yankee soldiers wrote home to his mother after that attack. He was the superstitious sort, you see, and the killing of the Wellingtons was said to be quite brutal. The soldier told his mother that the lady of the house swore the Yankees would never have their home. Her dying words have held true to this day. No one has ever been able to live here for long without being plagued by visions of the Wellington couple and their cook going about their daily lives as if they'd never been killed. Though these three ghosts have never done anyone any harm, they've not moved out either, and it's just been too unsettling for anyone to remain here more than a month or so."

The voice paused while others murmured.

"So it really is still their home," another voice spoke up.

The first voice had sounded like an older woman, and this new one seemed to belong to someone younger. Still I could see no one. My mind felt numb as it attempted to understand what was happening.

Suddenly Dalton's chair hit the floor with a crash as he stood up fast.

"What is going on?" he shouted, obviously as shaken as I by all this strangeness.

One of the unseen voices let out a scream.

"They must want us out of their home!"

That was a third voice, and it belonged to a man. As others gave murmurs of agreement, the crowd of people suddenly sprang into sight as if someone had parted a curtain behind which they'd been hiding. They were all dressed in odd clothes of the sort I'd never seen before. The women had skirts that were far too short for one thing, and some of them were even dressed as the men were!

That was so scandalous that I nearly forgot the shocking things they'd been saying and how we'd not been able to see them a mere second before. As we stared at them, they stared back at us, faces full of wonder. One woman came forward, hand out to touch my skirt. When she did, her hand passed right through the billowing layers of dark green fabric. That was when I at last understood. They had not been speaking awful lies. Somehow they were telling the truth.

I began to recall little pieces of our lives over the years that hadn't made much sense, but we'd just skirted around them for some reason. As if our minds could not process those inconsistencies that could have pointed out the fact that we were dead. For example, we'd not truly seemed to interact with Dalton's relatives who'd moved in after the war. Then there was the way none of them had told us goodbye when they'd left, and how we never had to send Nan out shopping for any sort of supplies. We just seemed to get by on what we had.

Somehow none of that mattered, though. We hadn't even realized we were dead, after all. We felt as though we still lived. And most important of all, no one had ever been able to have our home!

ABOUT THE AUTHORS

L. Michelle Cox

L. MICHELLE COX uses her collective twenty-two years of emotionally challenging nursing experiences to create impactful flash fiction pieces. A half-marathon finisher in 2014, Michelle uses exercise to stay physically and emotionally healthy. This novice author resides in Lexington, South Carolina, with her teenage son, Campbell. "Cam" and his older brother Mason, a US Army Infantryman, are the joys of her life, and are the inspiration behind this poignant story.

Richard D. Laudenslager

RICHARD D. "RICK" LAUDENSLAGER—artist, adventurer, explorer, builder, woodworker, entrepreneur, inventor, fantasy football enthusiast, ghost hunter, Bigfoot researcher, and, of course—writer.

Born in Quakertown, Pennsylvania May 17, 1966, his family moved to Lexington, South Carolina, when Rick was seven. An aspiring artist, he won the prestigious Burger King coupon in grade school for his poster about South Carolina wildlife. Then, as a commercial art student at Lexington High School he designed a logo that was selected for one of the first doc-in-a-box businesses in Columbia.

Laudenslager developed an affinity for comic books at an early age and was an avid collector for many years. His love of the comic book genre led to his endeavor to become a comic book artist and writer. Although that dream was abandoned in his twenties when the desire to pursue illustrating professionally left him, his interest in writing intensified, resulting in a lifelong quest to become a published author. He has a grown daughter he is very proud of. She is a graduate of The University of South Carolina and an art teacher.

You can reach the author with questions and comments about his work at his email address: RickL@TheBigfootTrap.com

Jenifer Boone Lybrand

JENIFER BOONE LYBRAND, born and raised in Lexington, South Carolina, is an avid reader who enjoys writing, photography, and art. Her mother, a devoted reader also, is credited for awakening the passion for reading in Jenifer at an early age. At any given time during her childhood, a multitude of books were available for reading and enjoying. In her early twenties, Jenifer began writing poetry for friends and relatives and continues to do so to this day.

Having experienced several unexplained events by the age of twenty, Jenifer became very interested in the supernatural and ghost stories, and began researching local legends and reading as many ghost stories as possible. Throughout her life, there have been many occasions where supernatural activities were sensed and witnessed, giving Jenifer an awareness for the paranormal that stoked her interest in writing ghost stories of her own.

Fran Rizer

FRAN RIZER'S magazine features have been published in *Better Homes & Gardens, South Carolina Magazine, Field & Stream, Southern Gardens, Living Blues, Bluegrass Unlimited, Bluegrass Now,* and others.

After retirement from teaching, she ventured into fiction and was a winner in the Augusta, Georgia, Porter Fleming Fiction Contest. Rizer's short fiction has been published in the USA and Canada, and her Callie Parrish mysteries have been nominated for SIBA and Agatha Awards.

The first three Callie Parrish novels were published by Berkley Prime Crime, a division of Penguin Books. Bella Rosa Books released the next three. Odyssey South Publishing brought out Rizer's first thriller, *KUDZU RIVER — A Novel of Abuse, Murder, & Retribution* as well as the seventh Callie Parrish mystery in 2015.

Rizer is a featured author on the SCETV series, *A Literary Tour of South Carolina,* on *Streamline* which is offered to all South Carolina public schools. Check out www.franrizer.com or see the Internet for links to interviews and reviews. She lives in South Carolina near her two sons, Nathan and Adam, and her grandson Aeden Rizer.

Nathan R. Rizer

NATHAN R. RIZER, a native of Columbia, South Carolina, served in the U.S. Navy in the Middle East before returning to South Carolina and earning a Bachelor of Science degree in Criminal Justice at the University of South Carolina. He is now an agent with the South Carolina Department of Probation, Pardon, and Parole.

Rizer and his teenaged son, Nathaniel Aeden Rizer, live in Lexington, South Carolina. Their interests include researching paranormal events, ghost hunting, and golfing. "Is It Me?" is Nathan R. Rizer's first published fiction.

J. Michael Shell

J. MICHAEL SHELL'S fiction has appeared in dozens of venues around the world, including the **Shirley Jackson Award** nominated *Bound For Evil* anthology (Dead Letter Press), the *Panverse Two All Novella Anthology* (Panverse Publishing), the '07 edition of the *Southern Fried Weirdness* anthology (Southern FriedWeirdnessPress)Hadley/Rille Books' *Footprints* a anthology, *Space and Time* magazine (USA),**Spectrum FantasticArtsAward** winning *Polluto* magazine (frequent contributor, UK), and *Tropic: The Sunday Magazine of the Miami Herald*, to name just a few.

His novel, *The Apprentice Journals* (Dog Horn Publishing, UK) came out in the summer of 2013, and the sequel *The Apprentice Journals II: Gemini* was just released! At the University of South Carolina (BA in English) Shell studied under James Dickey and William Price Fox.

Robert D. Simkins

ROBERT D. SIMKINS, born December 26, 1961, and raised in Florence, South Carolina, went to West Florence High School and then onto Clemson University where he received his Bachelor of Arts degree in Design in 1984. He started writing poems, songs, and stories as a teenager at the early age of thirteen. He continued writing songs and short stories during and after college. His interest grew into screenplay writing when he did a few gigs as an extra in movies being filmed in South Carolina. He went on to complete a full-length movie screenplay entitled "Murder of Innocence."

Simkins' career as an architect for the past thirty years has kept him busy but also has given him a visual platform to apply his artistic and creative point of view in the buildings he designs. His love of music and songwriting led him to join a rock and roll band many years ago to share his personal emotions and expressions. The band "Moonshine" was a great outlet for many years where he performed, wrote, and helped produce two full-length albums. Storytelling is his soul's passion and will always be the driving force in his life.

Robert D. Simkins resides in Northeast Columbia with his wife, Teresa, and has a grown daughter, Kristen, living in Cayce, South Carolina.

Two Ravens

TWO RAVENS is the pen name for husband and wife team Ciaran and Coal Corby. They have family in South Carolina, but thanks to their wanderlust currently reside in Oregon. They thoroughly enjoy horror and consider themselves honorary members of the Adams Family.

Previous publications include "Zombie Has Chills," a story in the *Through the Eyes of the Undead* anthology published by Library of the Living Dead Press. Under the pen name Ishamael, Coal has also had a series of nonfiction articles titled "Those Insightful Greeks" published in a Southern California newspaper called *The Messenger*, and these can still be viewed online.

www.ingramcontent.com/pod-product-compliance
Lightning Source LLC
Chambersburg PA
CBHW070839250626
47159CB00003B/852